A KIWI
BEFORE DYING

Also by Wendy Delaney

The Working Stiffs Mystery Series

Trudy, Madly, Deeply
Sex, Lies, and Snickerdoodles
There's Something About Marty
You Can't Go Gnome Again
Dogs, Lies, and Alibis
No Wedding For Old Men
Crazy, Stupid, Dead

A KIWI
BEFORE DYING

A WORKING STIFFS MYSTERY

BOOK 8

Wendy Delaney

Sugarbaker Press

Sugarbaker Press
PO Box 3271
Redmond, WA 98073-3271

This is a work of fiction. Names, characters, places, and incidents are a product of the author's imagination. Locales and public names are sometimes used for atmospheric purposes. Any resemblance to actual people, living or dead, or to businesses, companies, events, institutions, or locales is completely coincidental.

Cover by Lewellen Designs

Printed in the United States of America

A Kiwi Before Dying/Wendy Delaney – 1st edition, July 2021

ISBN: 978-0-9986597-6-3

For June
The spunky grandma I hope to be when I grow up.

Acknowledgments

The opening of this book was written in so many fits and starts during a very dark and isolating year that I had to set it aside for a while. There was too much death and dying going on in the real world for me to be able to write about a death in my fictional world. After a lot of encouragement from my pal and book previewer, Jody Sherin, who was eagerly waiting for more pages from me, and after many (many!) long walks, I stopped looking elsewhere for that happy place where I could write, because I wasn't going to find it doing what I had been doing. So I stopped focusing on baking the perfect loaf of sourdough, and sharpened my focus on this story and the characters I love. Within days I was writing again. Not great stuff and it often felt like pulling teeth, but it was forward progress. And Jody was always an email or a phone call away to cheer me on. Then midway through the completion of this book, I lost my biggest cheerleader and one of my best friends.

So Jody, thank you for every "You can do it" and "I love it, but fix this typo" that you gave me over the years. I don't know what I would have done without you. I still don't, but I know you're smiling with how this story turned out. I just wish I could have shared every page with you.

Big thanks to my friend and fellow author, Kathy Coatney, who said yes when I suggested a writing retreat so that I could bring this book across the finish line. Thanks also for all the great suggestions and for helping me make it through the last year.

Thanks as always to my resident "guy stuff" advisor, Jeff. Steve thanks you, too.

To "K," my "all things law enforcement-related" consultant, I'm always grateful for your kind assistance on the details that I really shouldn't rely on *Law and Order* to provide me.

Elizabeth Flynn, sock diva and editor extraordinaire, I can't thank you enough for helping me make my book the best it can be. Those butterfly print socks Harmony wore were for you.

Thank you, Maureen Butina, for letting me borrow Cliodhna's name. I was very happy to be able to use her lovely name on a featured character.

Amity and Killian were born during a brainstorming session with my Duke's Cafe Facebook group members. I knew I had something special in the names they had been christened with that night, and I so appreciate the kick-start the group's contributions gave the story.

Last but not least, I offer my heartfelt thanks to my dream team of beta-readers and supporters: Kathy Coatney, Heather Chargualaf, Lori Dubiel, Jan Dobbins, Brandy Lanfair-Jones, Susan Cambra, Cindy Nelson, Denise Fluhr, Vicki Huskey, Amber Lassig, Beth Rosin, Connie Lightner, Brenda Randolph, Christie Marks, Kath Maches, Donna Peterson, Rebecca Reitze, Renée Arthur, Beth Carpenter, Toni Mortensen, Mattie Piela, Deb Tysick-Hawrylyshyn, Patsy Hove, Melissa Hogan, Jenna Scully, Kris Spiess, Melanie McCready, Mary-Jane Grandinetti Rader, Deb Durham, Victoria Lewis, and Karen Haverkate. I'm very grateful to have you on Team Delaney.

Chapter One

"I still say she should have made the effort to be here," my grandmother grumbled, sticking her nose in an herb basket hanging near the register while I pulled out a credit card to pay for our Mother's Day brunch.

Gaylene Havens, the owner of the tea room with the adjoining garden center that Gram was eager to explore, shot her a nervous glance. "Is everything okay?"

Since it wasn't yet noon and my actress mother didn't "do" mornings, I wasn't surprised when she suggested that Gram and I stop by for coffee on our way home from Havens Berry Farm.

Marietta also didn't "do" the smell of farm country and would have been bored to tears with the Mother's Day sale Gram wanted to take advantage of, so everything about today's brunch at a table for two had been perfectly okay from my point of view.

"Unfortunately, my mother wasn't able to join us," I said while Gram scoffed.

I pointed at the blueberry scones in the glass display case behind the register. "But I'm sure she'd like a scone."

"Then she should have come with us to order one herself." Gram gave the bakery case a dismissive wave as she made tracks for a planter of lemon balm and mint.

"Better make it three scones." The more chewing we did at my mother's house, the less talking we'd have to do. If we combined quality pastry bliss with another caffeine fix, a good time should be had by all.

Maybe. If I was very, very lucky.

"You've got it," Gaylene said with a knowing smile as she rang me up. "Family dynamics can be *complicated* at times."

I handed her my card. "You have no idea."

Gaylene's gaze hardened as her adult son, Killian, clomped past me in heavy work boots and proceeded to clear the table Gram and I had just vacated with teacup-rattling gusto.

"Don't I?" Gaylene grimaced at the clatter of spoons striking her fine china. "Killian?"

The forty-year-old hunk in the backward baseball cap and dirty jeans bristled, looking more like a gangster gardener than a busboy. "What?"

His petite mother schooled her features as if she had just shifted into a cautious neutral to avoid making a scene in front of the seven remaining customers in her tiny cafe. "Maybe you should help your father for a while. With the plant sale, I'm sure he could use another pair of hands."

Killian vented a breath of annoyance. "Whatever you say."

Like a storm cloud, he rumbled back to the kitchen

with what I hoped would be minimal breakage, and I settled up at the register.

"You'll have to excuse him," Gaylene said, grabbing a white bakery bag for the scones. "He's been going through a rough patch."

In my family, "rough patch" was the term used for every time my mother returned home after a divorce, so I understood the context.

But since the news of Killian's divorce hit the local gossip circuit last summer and promptly morphed into Port Merritt's top story when his ex hooked up with his best friend, it was a safe bet that this particular patch had cut deep.

"I hadn't realized that Killian was back in town," I said as Gaylene handed me the bakery bag. And I couldn't imagine why he would want to return home now, three months after his ex-wife's wedding.

"Just for a little while. Until…" Censoring herself, she averted her gaze. "He knows how busy we are this time of year."

"Uh-huh." Since the berry farm's busy season wouldn't start until July, I didn't have to be the county prosecutor's body language expert to see that Gaylene didn't want to disclose whatever was really going on.

Returning my credit card, she flashed me a brittle smile. "Lovely to see you again, Charmaine. Be sure to remind your grandmother to visit our greenhouse. Tomatoes are half off today."

I recognized a polite dismissal when I heard one. And Gram needed no reminder as I discovered when I followed the path of stepping stones and found her pulling a vintage red wagon down the center of the plastic-covered greenhouse.

"Oh, good. Char, help me decide." Gram pointed at the two tomato plants in front of her. "The Early Girl or the Moskvich? Rory was telling me that his customers raved about their Moskvich harvest last summer."

Rory Havens took a break from watering the fuchsia baskets hanging near the entrance to give me a friendly wink. "And not just because I've got ten plants sitting here in need of good homes, and not very many buyers today."

Maybe because the farm supply store next door had a similar sale going on with eye-catching signs along the road to advertise it.

"I say get them both," I said, loading both pots onto the wagon. "Then you'll know which one to buy when we come back next Mother's Day."

"Ooh, a date for next year." Gram grinned. "How can I say no to that proposition?"

"Great. So are we ready to go?" Not that I was trying to rush her, but if we didn't leave soon, I could count on Marietta sending me a pouty text about being left all alone on Mother's Day.

And no one liked a pouty Marietta. Least of all me.

"What's over here?" Gram asked, walking toward a long row of herb flats.

Mr. Havens set down his hose and followed her down the brick paver walkway with the wagon. "Marjoram, oregano, chervil. You name it. We got it."

Gram turned to me. "I think I may need another wagon."

And since she'd be shopping for a while longer, I needed to call my mother to let her know that it would be another hour before we arrived. "No problem. Where are they?"

Mr. Havens waved me away. "Don't trouble yourself. Killian can bring you one. That's what kids are for—to fetch stuff, right?"

That felt like my cue to fetch the car that I'd had to park up the road when we first arrived to this popular Sunday brunch destination. "Absolutely. Take your time, Gram. While he gets you another wagon, I'm going to bring the car around." *And call Mom.*

"Sounds like a plan," she said, her eyes glazed like a kid's in a candy shop.

Searching my tote for my cell phone as I exited the greenhouse, I almost ran into Mr. Havens.

"Killian!" he called out repeatedly while a dog barked in the distance. "I swear that boy has trouble remembering that I'm paying him to actually do some work around here."

"Maybe he's in the kitchen." At least that was where Killian was when I saw him last. "If I see him I'll let him know he's needed back here."

But I didn't catch a glimpse of anyone but Gaylene and a few lingering customers on my way out through the garden center.

Outside, where a three-foot paddlewheel water feature mimicked a babbling brook, I looked up to soak in the warmth of the sun on what felt like a lovely preview of summer. Especially welcome after an almost solid week of misty rain, it helped Port Merritt live up to its sunny, blue sky reputation.

"Perfect." At least it would have been sans the neighborhood dog barking bloody murder about something.

For the sake of the dog and his owner, I hoped it was nothing more calamitous than a squirrel with the gumption to drink out of his doggy bowl. And I refocused my attention on the things that were great about today.

I had made the wonderful woman who raised me happy by bringing her to one of her favorite gardening destinations.

I had a dinner date scheduled with Steve, the man I loved.

And I had a bag of yummy scones swinging from my hand. Not much of a gift for the mother who excelled at having the best of everything, but maybe one of those fuchsia baskets would put a smile on her beautiful face. Plus, the price was right—way less than what it would cost me if I showed up with just the bag of carbohydrates that was mainly for me.

So scones and a fuchsia basket. "Yep, perfect," I said to myself as I crossed the berry farm parking lot to the deserted two-lane road.

Well, perfect except for the incessant barking that was sounding more like a distress call with every step I took. Making it impossible to ignore, because now there seemed to be a growing sense of urgency. And I knew in my bones that something was very wrong.

At first I thought there might be something going on at the barn-like veterinary clinic across the way. But judging by the increasing volume, I was closing in on the dog in trouble.

Was he next door on the farm supply grounds? Maybe tied up and managed to get himself into a terrible tangle while someone was shopping? Or worse, hit by a car and begging for rescue?

Shielding my eyes, I looked past the last few rows of raspberries but didn't have a clear view of anything beyond the copse of trees on the berry farm side of the property line.

With the mounting dread that I didn't have a minute to lose, I picked up my pace to the Subaru that I'd parked in a patch of weeds near the post and rail fence that bordered the Constantine Farm Supply property. Tossing the bakery bag and my tote on to the passenger seat, I took off in a run down a long, dirt drive, pebbles skittering under my sandals.

Halfway down the drive, with a grove of mature Douglas firs on my left and a red storage barn on my right, I had a clear shot of what appeared to be a reno-vated farm house. White two-story with forest green shutters maybe sixty feet back from the barn. A barking dog that I could hear but not see, and a new-model black pickup parked out front, but no sign that its owner was coming to the pup's rescue any time soon.

Then I saw movement and my heart tried to pound its way out of my chest.

It was a man stepping off the porch that wrapped

around the south side of the house—a man wearing a backward baseball cap.

He moved quickly, like he didn't belong there.

No wonder the dog was anxiously sounding the intruder alert.

My pulse pounding in my ears, I ducked behind the trunk of a giant cedar tree and cursed the fact that I had left my cell phone in the car.

What do I do? Go back and get it? Run next door and get Mr. Havens while I called 911?

No matter what, I was going to have to make a run for it, so I snuck a peek to see if the coast was clear.

Wait a minute. Is that...?

Not only did I recognize the guy, the canine alarm that had lured me back here was no longer blaring.

Instead, judging by the tail-wagging, it appeared that man and beast knew one another very well. And the man who had looked like a gangster just minutes earlier was smiling.

I didn't think I had ever seen Killian smile before. It looked good on him. But it made me feel like a dope, hiding behind a tree, so I stepped out and gave him a wave. "Is everything okay? I heard the barking and—"

"Everything's fine," he muttered, his face turning to stone while the shaggy mutt at the end of the leash in Killian's hand danced with excitement.

If everything was so fine, why had we both come to this dog's rescue? "What's going on?"

"Nothing."

I didn't believe that for a second. "So everything's

okay back here?"

"Yeah. Nothing you need to concern yourself with," Killian said, leading the dog toward the fence that separated this property from his father's berry farm.

It sure hadn't sounded that way to me. In fact, the way he was acting made me wonder what he'd been up to. "Your father's looking for you."

Passing the message along didn't earn me so much as a grunt of a response. But with Killian and the much happier dog disappearing behind the fence, I figured my civic duty had been fulfilled, and I returned to my original mission of retrieving the car.

When I went back inside to look for my grandmother, I spotted Mr. Havens standing by the entrance of the greenhouse.

He glared at Killian while the dog barked his own displeasure from the sprinkler pole his leash was looped around. "I guess I don't have to ask where you've been."

With his square jaw set, Killian clamped his mouth shut and stepped around his father.

"You had to pick today to do this," Mr. Havens said to his son's back.

"Leave it alone, Dad."

Mr. Havens turned to me after Killian rounded the corner. "Sorry about that. We usually have better manners around here."

I forced a smile. "No worries." Whatever was going on was none of my business.

Even though I was dying to know.

After Mr. Havens excused himself to help some customers at the garden center register, I spent the next ten minutes trying to coax my grandmother to join them with her two red wagons of herbs and veggies.

"I guess you're right. I've had enough fun for one day," Gram finally relented, following me out of the greenhouse.

That's when we heard the scream.

She turned to me, her eyes wide behind her silver-framed trifocals. "What the heck was that?"

I didn't know, but it came from the direction of that farm house, and probably had everything to do with a barking dog.

Chapter Two

A second white-and-green Chimacam County sheriff's SUV arrived at the farm house with lights flashing an hour later. The deputy parked next to Steve, the cop I had called after enough tearful accusations were hurled between screams for me to discern that the bloody body of Trevor Constantine had been discovered by his wife.

Killian's ex-wife.

The same Killian I had witnessed skulking around their house.

Based on the quick survey I had done of the Constantine Farm Supply employees and customers assembled in the back corner of the three-acre property, I was the only one who had seen anything around the probable time of the murder. Making me the only one of us who would be expected to testify if this came to trial.

Thinking about the charges that might be filed by my boss, the Chimacam County Prosecutor/Coroner, I swallowed the growing lump in my throat. Because she wouldn't be the least bit pleased when she found out that the investigating officers had to interview her assistant.

And I had thought that the only thing I had to worry

about today was being chewed out by a sulky mother for arriving late.

After almost two years of assisting with death investigations, at least I knew most of the players and what to expect from the next couple of hours.

Since Deputy Barnhart, first on the scene, didn't seem interested in talking to me beyond instructing me to not leave, I texted Marietta to let her know that a work thing had come up but I'd make it over there when I could.

Sort of true. The deputy coroner on duty this weekend would have been called by the sheriff, making my department officially involved. This would also add one more person to the list of those here who were less than thrilled to see me waiting to make a statement.

But topping the list had to be Killian Havens, shooting me a death stare from the weed-choked lawn, where he was sitting twenty feet away from me with the dog.

The only one who seemed oblivious to my presence was Amity Constantine, the wife of the victim, who had spent most of the last ten minutes sobbing into the broad shoulder of one of the guys Gram knew from the farm supply store.

While Deputy Barnhart inserted himself as a human shield between Amity and her ex-husband, Barnhart's partner thumbed for Killian to follow him toward the dog run at the rear of the house.

Amity stiffened as they passed. "Where are you going? Are you arresting him?"

Barnhart extended his hand like a traffic cop. "My partner's just going to ask him a few questions."

"I want him arrested!" Amity lunged, chunks of her pink-streaked blond hair the only part of her to achieve forward momentum when the deputy restrained her. "He killed my husband!"

"Please, ma'am. I know this is difficult, but—"

"He did it." Weeping, Amity pounded Barnhart's chest. "I know he did!"

After screaming a string of obscenities at Killian, Amity folded like soggy toast in Barnhart's arms, and he eased her to his SUV, where she collapsed into the passenger seat. Then he gave the Port Merritt Police detective standing next to me a look of entreaty.

All of us knew this was outside of Steve's jurisdiction, but since everyone there with a badge was waiting for the sheriff's detective to arrive, I wasn't surprised when Steve draped his arm around my shoulder and steered me toward the tree I had hid behind earlier.

But that didn't mean I had to enjoy the non-verbal directive to stand back while Deputy Barnhart cordoned off the scene with yellow tape. "What are you doing?"

Steve pulled me tight into his warmth. "You know exactly what I'm doing. And since you're just waiting to be interviewed as a witness, and nothing more," he emphasized as if I needed the reminder, "you can wait here. Better yet, go back to the tea room and keep your grandmother company until they call you."

Not a chance. "The nice officer over there told me not to leave, remember?"

Steve blew out a breath. "You would be two minutes away, and I'm sure your granny would appreciate—"

"You giving her a ride home? I'm sure she would." Which was why I called him in the first place. "Plus, Gaylene has more important things to do right now than babysit my grandmother." Namely, find her son a good lawyer, because he was going to need one.

Steve's dark eyes narrowed. "You promise to stay out of the way until your name is called?"

I squinted, trying to mirror his glare. "You mean like a *good* girl?"

"You know exactly what I mean."

"Uh-huh. I'll cling to this tree and not speak until spoken to."

"As much as I'd like to stick around and see that, I'll trust you to be on your best behavior." He planted a kiss on my lips. "It's okay if you want to be a bad girl after dinner, though."

"I'll take that under advisement," I said, trying to play it cool while my girl parts tingled with anticipation.

After waving good-bye to Steve, I killed a little time by taking a few photos of the growing crowd gathering on the front lawn. Not that I'd be interviewing any of them later, but I thought someone from my office might want to.

I was in the process of capturing a shot of the porch when I noticed a teenage girl standing on the other side of the back post and rail fence.

It seemed I wasn't the only one who noticed her, because the dog bounded toward her, his tail wagging with doggy joy when she reached through the fence to pet him.

So, you're friends, huh?

"Where were you when he was calling out for help earlier?" I muttered, lowering my cell phone when a frowning Deputy Barnhart came into sharp focus.

I had expected to be on the receiving end of some grief, but that didn't happen. Probably because Criminal Prosecutor Shondra Alexander, serving as this weekend's on-call deputy coroner, was pulling her white Mercedes into the spot Steve had vacated minutes earlier.

Popping the rear hatch of her SUV, she grabbed the black duffle everyone in my office referred to as the "bag of death" and then scanned the crowd like she wanted to shoot someone.

"It's not bad enough that I didn't get to spend Mother's Day with my sweet boy who served me a very nice breakfast in bed," Shondra said, training her glare on me as she approached. "I'm informed that one of the 911 calls came from you."

At six feet tall with the body mass index of a long-distance runner, this former cop from Texas turned heads by her sheer physical presence everywhere she went.

Today was no exception. Because it felt like everyone who had staked out a patch of grass near the house was watching, waiting for Shondra to stomp on me like an unwelcome ant at a picnic.

"I happened to be in the area when the woman who lives here started screaming. And it became obvious really fast that a call needed to be made."

Mainly because Amity Constantine had cried out the

magic word: *murder*.

Shondra narrowed her russet eyes. "Please tell me that's the extent of your involvement here."

If only I could. "I'm sort of a witness to her ex-husband being on the property around the possible time of the..." I didn't want to say "murder" or anything else that would make it sound like I'd inserted myself into what was about to become an official investigation. "Of whatever took place here. Because I was next door with my grandmother, and there was a barking dog, and I only came over because I thought he was hurt or something."

Uttering an expletive, Shondra started marching toward the house. "I really didn't need this today."

I had to run to keep up with her long strides. "I didn't go inside or touch anything."

"Thank the Lord for small mercies." She stopped in front of the crime scene tape and pointed back at the tree that had become my Constantine property hangout. "Wait over there and don't talk to anyone unless I'm with you. Understood?"

Like Steve, but in a much less pleasurable way, she couldn't have made herself more clear. "Yes, ma'am."

Shondra shifted her glare to the unmarked county vehicle pulling up next to her Mercedes. "About dang time," she muttered as Detective Jim Pearson climbed out.

He surveyed the scene much like she had moments earlier and then sauntered toward us with his own crime scene investigation duffle. "Sorry if I kept you waiting.

The kids and I were visiting their grandmother. You know...Mother's Day."

"Yeah. I know." Shondra gave me a look as if I bore some responsibility for ruining their afternoon and then lifted the yellow tape that stretched from Barnhart's vehicle to the kennel at the rear of the house. "Shall we?" she said to the detective while Amity and a balding jock who had an arm around her shoulder looked on.

I took that as my cue to resume hugging my tree. I then spent the next thirty-six minutes avoiding the stares of the curious onlookers while fielding calls from the mother who wanted to know what was keeping me.

Just as I was about to 'fess up and tell Marietta why I wouldn't be able to leave anytime soon, Shondra stepped off the porch and removed the blue nylon booties covering her sneakers.

"Let me call you back." Hoping I wouldn't get busted for using my phone, I dropped it into my tote and stood at attention as she headed for her car. "How'd it go in there?"

"As you might expect when you have a dead guy with a knife in his chest lying on a bloody kitchen floor. Oh, and a cat that decided to walk through our crime scene."

"Kitty prints?"

She nodded. "Everywhere. There was some food on a cutting board so that probably attracted her. Probably where the knife came from too."

"No human prints?" I asked, thinking about the work boots that I had watched Detective Pearson take from Killian and slip into an evidence bag while Shondra processed the scene.

"Nothing obvious. It's Pearson's case now, so he gets the honor of looking for 'em."

"So it's definitely a criminal case."

"With that knife sticking out of the victim?" Shondra's full lips twisted into a humorless smile. "Definitely."

I fell into step with her. "Now what?"

"Pearson will take your statement in a few minutes," Shondra said, opening the rear hatch and tossing in the duffle.

"A few minutes?" I looked over at the detective leading the newly widowed woman with the pink hair to a lawn chair, where she collapsed and buried her face in her hands.

Following my gaze, Shondra heaved a sigh. "Maybe more than a few."

Chapter Three

My mother dropped her scone to one of the fancy dessert plates she had set out on her dining room table. "It's certainly not the freshest pastry I've ever had."

"Do you want me to pop it into the microwave for a few seconds? That would revive it." If only I could nuke away the steady stream of griping she had been dishing out since my arrival.

Marietta broke off a bite-sized chunk and then inspected her fingers as if she'd chipped a nail from the effort. "It's fine."

It wasn't fine. Nothing about today had been fine.

A man had been killed.

It appeared that I was the only witness who saw someone on the property around the time of the murder.

And my mother was still fuming about being left alone for most of the day.

"I already said I'm sorry." And I knew there was nothing else I could say to make up for ruining the Mother's Day tea she'd prepared for Gram and me. "If I could have come earlier, I would have."

Marietta didn't look up from the crumbs she was rearranging on her plate. "I know."

"At least Gram was able to enjoy those pretty cucumber sandwiches you made."

She shrugged. "They looked a lot better four hours ago. Now they're dry."

"No, they're still good." I plucked a wedge from the serving platter at the center of the table and took a bite. The bread was stale and the limp cucumber slice she had cut too thin had no crunch, but I didn't want to make this crappy day worse by reminding the beautiful creature next to me about her lack of culinary skills. "But if you want to save any of these for Barry, we should probably put them in something airtight."

Barry was Mr. Ferris, my old high school biology teacher, who had taken a big leap of faith last year by becoming Marietta's fourth husband—probably the most impractical thing the lovestruck sap had ever done.

Despite my misgivings about my mother rushing into another marriage and moving back to Port Merritt, I had never seen her so happy.

Not so much with me at the moment, and there was little I could do to salvage the day beyond making the effort to rescue a few finger sandwiches.

But when I pushed away from the table to find a storage container, my mother placed her hand on mine. "Don't bother. I know when something is past its prime."

She wouldn't meet my gaze, so I knew we weren't talking about the sandwiches. "Did something happen that I don't know about?"

"I didn't get the part." She flashed me a tight-lipped

smile. "They wanted to go another direction."

"That can mean anything."

"*Younger*, Charmaine. It means younger."

"Maybe." Probably.

My fifty-seven-year-old mother frowned as much as her latest Botox injection would allow. "My agent said as much when he called."

"What did he say exactly?"

"He said the casting director was an idiot and that I should enjoy my Mother's Day. You know, all the right things to cushion the blow without saying much of anything. The story of my life today." She shot me a frosty glare. "No one's telling me much of anything."

And that was the way it needed to stay. "If you're referring to—"

"Your grandmother said something happened near where you had brunch—something bad. That's the work thing that you texted me about, right? But she refused to say anything else."

Thank you, Gram.

I wasn't supposed to discuss the murder and had asked my grandmother to keep a lid on everything she'd heard so that when the news hit the local gossip circuit we wouldn't be quoted as anyone's news source. "There isn't—"

"You two always keep me out of the loop, and I must say that I resent being excluded, especially today of all days."

"Then maybe you should have accepted my brunch invitation."

"You sound like my mother."

I shrugged. "Well? It's true."

Marietta folded her arms under her double Ds. "And you know very well that I fast until noon."

Slept until noon was more like it.

This conversation was getting me nowhere I wanted to go, and I had a hot date with a hot cop that I needed to get ready for.

I made a show of picking up my cell phone. "Oh, look at the time. I should—"

"You just got here." She snatched the phone from my hand as if she were taking away a favorite toy. "What you should do is talk to your mother."

So much for making a clean getaway.

Staring out the picture window in her dining room, I focused on an azalea bush in brilliant pink bloom while racking my brain for a safe subject to discuss. "Did Gram tell you about the tomato plants she bought? If those babies all ripen at the same time, she's gonna have tomatoes coming out of her ears."

"Fascinating. So tell me." Marietta set my phone down and leaned in. "What the heck happened that kept you busy all day?"

"Nothing that I can talk about."

She sucked in a breath. "Because someone died."

Crap. I nodded.

"And not from natural causes, I assume."

"Uh... all I can tell you is that a body was discovered and I couldn't leave."

"Because you're some sort of death investigator?" Her

eyes widened. "I didn't think you had the kind of job where you have to look at dead bodies."

"I don't. I just had to stay and wait for the people who do have that job to show up."

"Whatever for?"

"Because they wanted to talk to me." I stole my phone back. "Now can we drop this, please, because I have to go."

"You know what this reminds me of," she said with a dreamy look in her green eyes. "The episode of *Peachtree Girls* where I was working undercover and discovered the dead body in the pool. Totally blew my cover when I testified at the trial. I did enjoy those scenes with Davy what's-his-name who guest-starred as our victim. Lovely man. Smelled delightful."

I had no desire to reminisce about her old TV show. "I'm sure he made an excellent dead guy, but—"

"Oh, mah!" Marietta exclaimed, slipping back into the southern accent she had used on her Atlanta-based show. "I just put two and two together. You're the one who discovered the body!"

"Nope, and there was no pool."

"Well, you were there and must have seen something. That's why they wanted to talk to you, right?"

"I really can't get into it."

"Because you're a witness." She pointed a tapered index finger at me. "That's why you had to stay. You *saw* something!"

Crap. Crap. Crap.

I got to my feet. "I can *not* talk about this and would

appreciate you not repeating a word of this to anyone else."

"Repeating what? You barely told me anything."

"There's a good reason for that, and it has everything to do with me wanting to keep my job. That's why this conversation can't go any further."

"Fine." My mother gave me a three-fingered salute like a good Girl Scout. "I promise I won't say anything. Although I'm sure it will come out eventually. You know how it is around here. No one can keep a secret."

Especially about something this juicy.

"Then again, if no one else saw you there, you shouldn't have anything to worry about, right?" she asked, watching as I cleared the table.

"I wasn't the only one there."

"Oh. Then, sugar, you're doomed. 'Cause this is going to spread like wildfire."

That was what I was afraid of.

Chapter Four

"You sure you wouldn't rather go to Port Townsend?" Steve asked, raising his voice to be heard over the Def Leppard classic blasting our eardrums as we stepped into Eddie's Place. "Since you got dressed up, I thought white tablecloths and a little less volume might be in order."

I batted my freshly mascaraed eyelashes while a cacophony of rumbling balls and scattering pins in the adjoining eight-lane bowling alley thundered behind us. "Why? Because you want to woo me with sparkling conversation?"

"Uh-huh." He scanned the crowd occupying most of the tavern's tables, offered a chin salute to a cop buddy raising a glass, and then Steve zeroed in on the closest flat screen with the baseball game he had been watching at my house.

"That's what I thought." Taking his hand, I led Steve to our usual seats at the end of the polished oak bar, where he could watch the rest of the game. "I want to wish Rox a happy Mother's Day." And find out if she had heard any news about the murder.

Roxanne and Eddie Fiske were two of our best friends since childhood. Since giving birth seven months ago, Rox had been on a limited work schedule here at the red brick warehouse they had converted into one of Port Merritt's favorite eateries. I often filled in for her behind the bar on the weekends, which worked out great for her and the baby, and earned me tips for gas money, but had cut our time to hang out to a minimum. So I was happy to see her emerge from the kitchen with a couple of pizzas.

But if Rox was the one delivering pizza orders during the dinner rush, that typically meant that someone hadn't shown up for work.

"Hey," I called out when she raced by without acknowledging my presence. "Are you by yourself out here?"

She cut me a withering glance that told me everything I needed to know.

"That's not good," Steve said, his breath warm on my ear as we took our seats.

While waiting for Rox to finish filling a pitcher of beer for a guy in a red and white bowling league shirt, I looked around for Eddie.

No Eddie. No bar waitress either, adding to today's "not good" factor.

"Where is everyone?" I asked a flush-faced Rox when she slapped a couple of coasters in front of us.

"Eddie's working on a pesky pin-setter. Vince took the day off to visit his mom. Carlos is in the kitchen pumping out orders as fast as he can, and I, your favorite bartender, am at your service."

"And where's Libby?" The server I had worked with last weekend.

Rox narrowed her cocoa brown eyes. "Libby quit. No notice. Showed up a couple of hours ago to announce that she was moving to Seattle with some guy and then walked out the door."

This day just kept getting better and better. "You should have called me. I would have helped out."

"I figured you had enough on your plate." She leaned in. "You know, because of what happened to Trevor Constantine."

Yep, she'd definitely heard the latest news.

Arching an accusatory eyebrow, Steve turned to me.

"Knock it off with the eyebrow thing, because she didn't hear it from me," I protested.

Rox glanced over at one of the more senior regulars taking a seat near the register. "Leah mentioned it when she picked up a big order for the family."

The name sounded vaguely familiar. Did I remember her from high school? "Leah?"

"A cousin, I think. Worked with Trevor and said she saw you talking to the police." Rox thumbed toward the other end of the bar. "You'll have to tell me all about it after I deal with a few thirsty customers. You two want the usual?"

I nodded and after Steve rattled off the name of one of the drafts on tap, he slid off the barstool. "I know you know this, but you really don't have to tell her all about it."

"I have no intention to." Because I didn't want to become a bigger part of this story than I already was.

He kissed my cheek. "Good girl. I'm going to see if Eddie needs a hand. Order whatever kind of pizza you want as long as it's a large with sausage and pepperoni."

In other words, his favorite combo with the extra cheese I'd be adding so that it could also be my favorite.

"So what happened out there?" Rox asked when she delivered our drink order a minute later. "Leah made it sound like trouble had been brewing between Killian and Trevor for a long time. You know...because of Amity. Sort of a 'two dogs and one bone' thing."

Yeah? Then Leah knew more about what led up to the murder than I did.

"I have no idea. I was there only because I took my grandmother to brunch at the berry farm. Which reminds me..." I pulled a large white envelope from my tote and slid it across the counter. "With everything going on today it may not feel very happy, but happy Mother's Day."

Her face split into a grin. "Awww, thank you. I've been so busy here I almost forgot about it."

I sipped the glass of chardonnay she'd brought me while she opened the card.

"I love this picture," Rox said, referring to the image on the front of a young mom with big hair and a baby in her arms. "It reminds me of my mother."

"I thought it might." Since that was who I had thought of when I spotted the card at the drug store yesterday.

Rox sucked in a breath. "My mother! I forgot that I was supposed to pick up Alex at six so that my sister could take her out to dinner. What time is it?"

I checked the time on my phone. "Almost six. If you hurry, you can make it."

"Not until Eddie takes over here." She winced. "I hate to ask, but would you find Eddie and—"

"No need. I've got this," I said, coming around to the other side of the bar.

"Are you sure?" She looked at the black wrap dress I'd thrown on for tonight's date. "I don't want to ruin your evening."

I shooed her away. "Go. Pick up your kid and enjoy the rest of your Mother's Day."

"You're the best." She gave me a warm squeeze, provided a quick update about the tabs being run, then grabbed her purse and dashed past the jock I had seen consoling Amity a few hours earlier.

Another cousin coming here to eat or drink away his sorrows? A friend of the family? I wished Leah was still here for me to ask.

Stealing peeks at him and his date as I weaved my way through the crowd to take drink orders and clear dishes, I didn't get the sense that the guy recognized me. Then again, he only seemed to have eyes for the curvy brunette he was with.

And they seemed to be in such deep conversation that I hesitated to approach them, especially when I saw him pull a napkin from the dispenser on the table and wipe his eyes.

After checking in at a nearby table, I turned to greet them, but the brunette cut me off with a sad smile while the jock stared out the window at a motorcycle pulling out of the parking lot. "We'll need a few minutes," she said, waving me away with a hand adorned with an expensive-looking engagement ring.

"Of course," I said, feeling a little guilty that I had intruded upon their grief. Not so guilty, though, that I regretted being dismissed so that I couldn't listen in on a snippet of their conversation.

I headed back toward the bar where Steve stood, watching me with a beer in his hand. "I take it Eddie didn't need your help."

"Nope, but when Rox told him she was leaving to pick up the kid, I thought you might."

On a busy night like this he thought right. "Good. Put down the beer and take these into the kitchen." I shoved the short stack of dirty dishes at him the second he had two free hands. "And bring out any orders that Carlos has ready and then make the rounds with some menus."

"You know you're hot when you're bossy."

Words like that made me want to eat the man up with a spoon. "Maybe I should order you around more often."

"I'm here to serve." Steve's mouth stretched into a sexy smile. "Literally."

"And don't think that I don't appreciate it."

"You can show me just how much you appreciate it a little later," he said, bumping the kitchen door open with his hip.

With my cheeks warming at the thought of the fun

waiting for us, I filled drink orders while singing along with a Belinda Carlisle hit from my childhood.

Between the upbeat music and the good mood Steve had put me in, I was almost able to forget about the murder. Until I slipped out from behind the bar to deliver those drinks and saw the brunette motioning me to their table.

"Are you ready to order?" I asked, pasting my best customer service smile on my face to counter the grim expression on the jock slanting a glance at me.

"I think so." She pointed at the top of the laminated menu's sandwich column. "We're going to share one of these grinders."

"I told you I don't want it," he grunted, folding his beefy arms.

"Baby, you need to eat something." Her dark blue eyes glittered with tears as she watched him from across the table. "Drink something too. What's that IPA you like?"

He didn't respond and with each second that ticked by it looked like the emotional dam she had been trying to hold back might burst, so I suggested Eddie's most popular pale ale on tap.

She handed me the menus. "Fine."

"Anything for you? Maybe some water?" She looked like she could use some.

"Sure. Where's the restroom?" she asked, her voice mainly breath as she got up from her bench seat.

"This way." I glanced over my shoulder.

Almost as tall as me in my two-inch slingbacks, I

guessed the woman following me to be five-seven and somewhere in her late twenties.

I slowed so that I could see her face. "Are you okay?"

She shook her head. "It's been a rough day."

"I hear you there." *And wish that I could ask you about how you knew Trevor.*

After pointing out the ladies' room door to the left of the bar, I looked up to see Steve scowling at me as he cleared a table.

"What?" I mouthed to him.

Shaking his head, he approached with a plastic tub of dirty dishes. "You know what."

"I have no idea what you're talking about."

"Give them some space so they can grieve in peace."

"I'll have you know that I was merely trying to provide good customer service."

Steve smirked. "Sure you were."

I didn't care about the smirk as much as I wanted to hear how he knew they were grieving, and fell into step with him as he headed for the kitchen. "Who are they? Do you know them?"

"You don't recognize Joel Stillwell?"

I remembered him as a skinny teenager from the summers I worked at my great-uncle Duke's diner. "That's Joel Stillwell?" Today's version of him—with a lot less hair and fifty pounds of muscle packed onto his once-lanky frame—bore little resemblance to the boy I used to think was pretty cute. "I never would have guessed that."

I followed Steve through the swinging kitchen door.

"Who's that with him?" I shouted to be heard over the baseball play-by-play blaring from the radio at Carlos's workstation.

Steve set down the plastic tub with more force than necessary. "How should I know?"

"Well, you seem to make it your business to know most everyone around here."

He turned to loom over me. "Hey, I'm not the one trying to milk them for information."

While I sputtered with as much righteous indignation as I could muster, Carlos looked from me to Steve and then back to me. "Something going on out there that I need to know about?"

I handed him the order ticket for the grinder. "Everything's okay. There's just someone who's upset about something."

"About their order?" Carlos asked, his eyes wide.

"No, no." With Steve here I knew I had better choose my words carefully. "Someone they know passed away today and—"

"Trevor Constantine, right?" Carlos inched closer, lowering his voice. "I heard he was murdered."

"No comment," Steve answered for me.

But I wanted to find out what else Carlos had heard. "Who told you that?"

"My girlfriend, Paige." He pulled a large pizza from the oven while he talked. "She's tight with Amity. Been over there most of the day."

Oh, yeah?

After slicing the pizza into wedges, he slid it onto an

aluminum pan and handed it to me, which I promptly passed to Steve so that I could talk to Carlos without interruption from my self-appointed censor. "Deliver this to the group of guys in the bowling shirts and keep an eye on the bar for a minute." I smiled sweetly. "Please and thank you."

Steve grunted. "In other words, get out."

He knew me too well. "I just need to wash my hands."

"Sure." Scowling, he swung the kitchen door open. "One minute. Then I'm coming back to haul your prying butt out of here."

Without a second to lose, I turned back to Carlos. "So your girlfriend knows Amity pretty well?"

He smiled with pride. "Was the maid of honor at her wedding."

Then it was a safe bet that Carlos had spent some time with the Constantines. "Did you know Trevor?"

"We weren't buds like the girls, but yeah, I knew him," Carlos said while he sprinkled shredded cheese on the two pizzas on his worktable.

"How about Joel Stillwell? You know him?"

"Sure. A couple years back I worked with him at his dad's shop."

If Carlos could build custom cabinets, I wondered why he had opted to sweat over a hot pizza oven instead.

"Mainly doin' installations. Then Joel left to do his own thing, and the old man decided to sell the business." Carlos flashed me a rare smile. "Heck, if I could spend the rest of my days fishin' I'd do the same thing."

That explained why the Stillwell Woodworks building

out on Route 17 had turned into an automotive supply store shortly after I moved back to town. Also why the avid angler in front of me now worked nights.

Carlos turned to me. "Why are you asking about Joel?"

I pointed at the order for the grinder. "That's for him and someone he's with, and—"

"Oh, man." Wiping his hands on a towel, Carlos ran to the door. "Why didn't you say so?"

"Because I didn't know you knew him," I called after him, my voice unable to compete with the tavern's decibel level once I stepped within thirty feet of a speaker.

A guy sitting in front of me looked up to ask for a refill. "And we need some menus if that's not too much of an inconvenience," his date huffed as if I had placed my tip in jeopardy by not being at her beck and call for the last couple of minutes.

After I assured her that I'd be right back and greeted a couple of new arrivals, I returned to my post behind the bar where I found an equally annoyed Steve.

"About time," he grumbled when I reached past him for the handle of his favorite draft on tap. "Two of the ladies in the corner want lemon drops, whatever that is."

"No problem." I didn't have the recipe memorized, but I knew where I could find it. "I'll deliver this beer. You grab the mixed drink bible from under the cash register." Which provided me a few precious seconds to find out why Carlos was waving me over from the end of the bar.

Carlos pointed at the amber brew in my hand. "Is that

for Joel?"

What? "No." I did a mental head slap. "I got side-tracked after I took his order." *In the kitchen, talking to you.* "You go and make their sandwich and I'll get his drink. What about his ladyfriend? What's her name again?" I asked, hoping he'd fill in the blank.

"Brooke. She said you were bringing her a water."

Brooke. Thank you, Carlos! "It'll be coming right up."

And then I planned to find out what he knew about their connection to Trevor Constantine.

Chapter Five

After Eddie relieved me at the bar around eight, I spent the last hour of Carlos's shift trying to get the skinny on who was who in Trevor's life.

Carlos had never been chatty in the best of circumstances, so the few details he was willing to offer up sounded razor-thin. And what little I managed to glean about the Constantines and the family business had clearly been colored by what Amity confided to Carlos's girlfriend, Paige.

The third-hand information came across as sour grapes that didn't contain enough juice to make the rounds on the local gossip circuit. With the possible exception of some family squabble that resulted in Amity not being on speaking terms with the majority of her in-laws.

"I never saw Trevor have a beef with anyone, though. Neither did Joel," Carlos said while he wiped down an aluminum counter.

I started the dishwasher I had just finished loading and turned back to give Carlos my full attention. "He told you that?"

He shook his head. "He can't believe this any more than I can. It just doesn't make sense that someone would murder the dude. I mean sure, the business has to be worth some money, but..."

"But?"

"I didn't think that Amity was serious."

I stepped closer, the hair prickling at the back of my neck. "Serious about what?"

"About getting him to sell."

This was news to me. "The Constantines are selling?"

Carlos gave me a hard look. "*Trevor* was. The business was his baby. Has been ever since he inherited it from his dad last year."

That would have been right before he hooked up with Amity. Which was some interesting timing.

"You want this?" Carlos held up a white pizza box containing a large sausage-mushroom combo that never got picked up. "Paige is sick of me bringing home pizza, and I doubt that Amity is gonna feel like eating."

I took that to mean that Amity had been spending the evening at his and Paige's house while a team from the sheriff's department worked the murder scene.

I had assumed that Amity would have been taken under the broad-shouldered wing of the Constantine family member I'd seen her with while we all waited to be interviewed. Either that comfort port in this emotional storm wasn't truly available to her, or Amity was making a conscious choice to keep her distance from him.

"Sure, thanks," I said, taking the cardboard box from Carlos. I knew Steve would be too hungry to care that its contents had been sitting around for a couple of hours. I also knew that he would become very cranky about how this dinner date had devolved if I were to join him at the bar empty-handed.

With a nod, Carlos grabbed a garbage bag and headed for the dumpster by the side door.

"Wait," I said, calling after him.

The stony set of his jaw told me he was a man who was all talked out for the night. Which was completely understandable. But I didn't want any more dirt from him, at least not tonight. Quite the opposite.

"I'd appreciate it if you didn't mention our conversation to your girlfriend or Amity." Especially Amity.

I couldn't leave it there. Not when I had inside knowledge about the bloody mess she'd soon be going home to.

"Have her give me a call, though, if she needs some help…" I wasn't sure how graphic I needed to get. "You know, with the cleanup. I know of a couple of companies through the coroner's office." Mainly because I'd been on the receiving end of the "Who's going to clean this up" question enough times in the field to have an answer at the ready.

Grimacing, Carlos pulled out his cell phone and took down my number. Then he muscled the black plastic bag out the door as if I had just added to his burden.

I knew I had. Just as I knew that I shouldn't get any more involved in the death of Trevor Constantine than I already was.

"What the heck is going on in here?" Steve asked as

the side door banged shut behind Carlos.

I swung around with the pizza box in my hands like an offering. "Nothing much." *That you need to know about.*

"I thought you were going to make us something to eat, and that looks suspiciously like a leftover pizza." Steve opened the box. "With a whole lot of mushrooms."

"Don't worry. There's a layer of sausage in there so you'll hardly taste them."

"Uh-huh." He flicked a few to the side as if to satisfy himself that I wasn't trying to sneak a vegetarian pizza past him, and then grimaced. "It's barely warm."

I shut the lid on his fingers. "It'll be hot in no time. I just need to pop it in the microwave."

"Not so fast." Steve pulled the box from my clutches and headed for the sink. "We need to scrape off some fungus first."

I reached my arms around him to stop his progress. "A few vegetables aren't going to kill you."

"Says you."

"What are you two up to?" Eddie asked, angling past us on his way to the sink with a tub of dirty bar glasses.

"Nothing," I repeated, hating the burn in my cheeks as I jumped off Steve's back.

"Doesn't look like nothing." Eddie smirked. "I'll have you know that I can't have my employees doing whatever it is you kids are doing in my kitchen."

Steve tossed the box to the counter. "And I'll have you know we're not your employees."

"Oh, yeah." Eddie slapped his shoulder. "In that case,

carry on."

"You heard the man," Steve said, pulling me back into his arms the second the kitchen door swung shut behind Eddie.

"Hey, I thought you were hungry."

His brown eyes darkened like molten chocolate as he pressed me close. "You thought right."

Oh.

I locked my fingers behind his neck and angled for a kiss. "Carry on, then."

⁂

The next morning, I arrived at the third-floor courthouse office of the Chimacam County Prosecutor to find it buzzing with the news of Trevor Constantine's murder. Mainly because Jan, our receptionist, had pulled into the farm supply store parking lot when Detective Pearson arrived, where she saw me waiting to be interviewed.

Dang it.

Before I'd had a chance to say good morning to the administrative staffers huddled around Jan's desk, I found myself fending off more rapid-fire questions than Marietta at her last press junket.

One of the office gossipmongers closed in on me. "Holy cow, Char. You actually saw Killian Havens fleeing the scene?"

Crap. Could Jan have made the situation I found myself in sound any worse than it already was?

There was no way I could set them straight without

getting into the details of the statement I provided. And if I wanted to keep my job, that wasn't an option.

"I can't talk about it. Sorry," I said without slowing.

Ignoring the disappointment aimed at my back, I rounded the corner to beat a hasty retreat and spotted my boss emerging from her office with Shondra in the lead.

Shondra's laser-like glare as Frankie Rickard stood outside her doorway and called out my name told me everything I needed to know about the meeting that had just concluded.

My presence at the crime scene had been no small part of Shondra's debrief with the county prosecutor.

I had expected as much, especially since I knew my statement would make an appearance in Detective Pearson's report once he completed his investigation.

What I hadn't expected, after a mostly sleepless night, was a summons to Frankie's office before I could slip into the breakroom and steel myself with another jolt of caffeine.

With a lump lodged in my throat, I felt as welcome as a dog fart as Shondra stalked past without so much as a side-long glance.

Something was up.

She didn't think that I had said anything to Jan about Killian, did she?

"Well?" Patsy, Frankie's long-time legal assistant, looked over her computer monitor and aimed her pointed chin at me. "She has a meeting with the mayor to get to, so don't just stand there."

Easy for Patsy to say. No one in this office was trying to squeeze her for information about a murder.

After a couple of deep breaths, I gripped the door frame of Frankie's office and prayed that whatever admonition I was going to get would be quick and from a distance.

After all, she was in a hurry with an important meeting to rush off to.

Glancing up from her desk chair, a cool smile flashed across Frankie's peony pink lips. "Close the door please, Charmaine."

Dang. So much for rushing.

I clicked the door shut and approached the sixty-something woman folding her hands on the manila file folder in front of her.

I didn't doubt for a second that it had been hand-delivered by Shondra minutes earlier.

Instead of inviting me to take a seat in one of the high-backed Georgian chairs across from her desk, Frankie's gaze tightened behind her wireframe bifocals. "Shondra filled me in on yesterday's unfortunate events. You understand that you might be called as a witness."

"Yes, ma'am." I also understood the subtext: Keep my mouth shut. "And I haven't talked to anyone about it since my interview with Detective Pearson." If we didn't include my conversation with Carlos last night.

She nodded. "It might be tough to keep it that way since it's all anyone around here wants to talk about. So it might be best if you keep a low profile outside of the office today."

This sure wasn't what I had expected to hear, but... "Okay."

"Shondra will have a subpoena ready for delivery in about an hour, and Patsy has a few errands you can run, so that should keep you busy for a good chunk of the day."

"What about the rest of the day?"

Frankie peered at me over her bifocals. "Just keep that low profile I mentioned."

"Got it."

"Oh, and Charmaine," she said, stopping me before I reached the door. "Since this is the biggest news story we've had around here for some time, don't be surprised if someone calls you for an interview."

"Hardly anyone there knew who I was, so I doubt—"

"Jan's cousin works for the *Gazette* and was with her on Sunday. So, like I said, don't be surprised."

Swell.

Chapter Six

After driving to Seattle to hand-deliver that subpoena to a nice lady who had the bad timing to be in town to witness the armed robbery of a gas station, I had an hour to kill before the next ferry back to Port Merritt. I also had a growling stomach, so I pulled into the parking lot of a nearby sub shop for a sandwich to go.

That's when my cell phone rang.

I didn't recognize the number but picked up in case it was about work.

"Is this Charmaine?"

She sounded too eager to speak with me, much like I'd expect from a reporter tracking down a lead.

"Yes," I said without masking my irritation that Jan gave her cousin my number. Not only that, but this chick had such an annoyingly breathy lilt to her voice that she reminded me of my mother.

"Uh...is this a bad time to talk?"

This was as good a time to shut her down with a firm *no comment* as any. "What's this about?"

"Carlos Campana gave me your number and..."

Argh. This wasn't a reporter. Amity Constantine was

the caller breathing in my ear.

While I stifled a full-body cringe, Amity introduced herself and then proceeded with some rapid-fire bitching about the condition the police left her kitchen in.

I didn't make much out of it. If I were to suddenly lose Steve, I'd be mad at the world, too.

Amity paused to replenish her air supply. "Anyway, Carlos mentioned that you could help me out."

"I'd be happy to." I reached into my tote for my notebook with the cleaning service contact information.

"Awesome," she chirped, shifting from indignant to upbeat so quickly she was giving me mental whiplash. "When can you get here?"

She wanted to meet in person? Not at all what I had expected to hear, but given how this call had started out, what was one more surprise?

I dropped the notebook. "To your house or Carlos's?"

"Mine. I'm home now, and would like to get this over with today if possible."

Based on how Shondra had described the bloody scene, I was sure that was the case. I was also intrigued about seeing it for myself. So if the victim's wife needed some one-on-one consultation so that she could move on with her life, who was I to say no? Especially on a day when I wasn't supposed to rush back to the office.

I added a half hour of driving time from the Port Merritt ferry dock. "I could be there around three, if that works for you."

"Perfect! See you then."

Again, way too cheery. But maybe Amity Constantine

was a woman with a talent for compartmentalizing her grief.

I could hardly wait to get back to town to find out.

I had underestimated how long it would take for the packed ferry to unload. Fortunately, traffic was light enough to allow me to pass the horse trailer poking along on Route 104, and I made it to the Constantines' farm house with two minutes to spare.

The black pickup and a flashy red Corvette that I recognized from yesterday were parked in front of the house, making me wonder if these were "his and her" vehicles.

After pulling into the spot that Shondra had last occupied, I crawled out of my car and heard some all too familiar barking.

Like yesterday, the home canine alarm system was blaring. This time, while restrained by the thirty-something widow at the front door.

Leaning over with one hand wrapped around his collar, Amity projected emotional control, as opposed to the first glimpse I'd had of her. She also appeared indifferent to the peep show she was giving me of her braless breasts under her snake print V-neck.

"Hello," I said with a wave as I approached the porch. "I'm Charmaine."

Amity squinted at me through slits formed by swollen eyelids. I'd experienced a sleepless night of ugly crying when my husband dumped me for a TV gig in New York, so I recognized the shattered look. But it sure didn't fit with how perky she had sounded on the phone, and it gave me second thoughts about what I was getting myself into. Especially when the dog by her side started growling.

"I know you. You were here yesterday," Amity stated, holding him close with an arm sporting a pretty peacock feather tattoo. "You didn't mention that on the phone."

I felt tempted to remind her that she had been the one who wanted to meet. But instead I forced a smile and pointed at her dog. "I was parked on the street and heard this one barking so frantically that I thought he might be hurt. That's the only reason why..."

Standing barefoot in skinny jeans ripped at the knees, Amity's gaze raked over me while I wrestled with how much I should admit to witnessing.

"You're the one who saw Killian." Her voice was barely more than a whisper as if she were having trouble wrapping her brain around her words.

I nodded, not wanting to add anything that would set off another explosion of accusations against her ex-husband.

She chewed on her lip for a second. "Huh."

Again, not the reaction I had anticipated.

"We have a lot to talk about then," she said, stepping back from the doorway with the dog.

I figured that was as much of an invitation to enter her home as I was going to get, and followed Amity inside.

Curling up with the dog on a natty mocha sofa, she motioned for me to take the easy chair to her left. "I'd offer you some coffee or something but I haven't been able to step into the kitchen since..."

The mutt rested his head on her thigh as if he sensed that she needed the emotional support, leaving me to fill the awkward silence between us.

"I'm fine." Or I would be once I got this over with.

Crossing a braided oval rug, I did a quick scan of the living room. The walnut paneled walls and yellowing lace doilies on the chair I had been directed to didn't fit with this chick's style, and made me feel like we were both visitors to this house.

A picture window with Roman shades drawn halfway bathed the space in soft light while providing a view of Havens Berry Farm for the smoky brown and white cat basking on the ledge. I assumed the same one that had left the bloody kitty prints that Amity wasn't eager to look at.

Not that I could blame her.

No sooner did my butt sink into the chair cushion, the cat crossed the hardwood floor and sprang onto my lap.

"Shoo her away if she bothers you," Amity said, running a graceful hand over one of her dog's floppy ears.

She had already curled into a fluffy ball and was purring, making me envy her comfort level. "She's fine."

Amity nodded, setting her pink-streaked ponytail into motion. "So..."

I fixed a polite smile on my face and waited while she gave me a hard stare.

Pressing her lips together, she cleared her throat as if she were having trouble finding her voice. "What exactly did you see yesterday?"

"I didn't see anyone leaving the house, if that's what you're asking." Which was what I would want to know if my ex-husband had been spotted at the scene of a murder.

"But I thought you saw Killian—"

"On the porch, and for just a second."

Amity's swollen eyes widened as if I were telling her a ghost story. "Then what happened?"

"Then he stepped off and went to this guy." I pointed at the furry mutt occupying most of the space to her right. "Who seemed very happy to see him."

"That's it?"

I didn't see any point in mentioning I had been cowering behind a tree during all this. "That's it."

"Then you really didn't see anything."

Considering her dead husband was lying in a pool of blood at the time, I wouldn't have put it that way. "Just what I told you." And the sheriff's detective.

A bubble of laughter escaped Amity's lips a split second before she buried her face in her dog's ruff.

What the heck?

Was it simply honest relief that I was in no position to accuse anyone of murder?

Nervous laughter at the situation she found herself in because she had no more tears to shed?

Whatever it was, it didn't jibe with yesterday's fury launched toward her ex.

Straightening, Amity cleared her throat again, making her face as blank as a new canvas. "Okay, then," she announced with the cheery tone I'd heard on the phone. "About your cleaning service..."

I had been zeroing in on the steel she had injected into her jaw to keep her emotions in check, and wasn't sure I heard her right. "I'm sorry. What?"

"Your services. How much do you charge?"

My services? "I think there's been a misunderstanding," I said over the barking that erupted when someone knocked at the front door. "I—"

"Sorry. Let me get that." Pushing off the sofa, she caught up to the dog. "Max, quiet."

From my seat I had a clear shot of Amity holding Max by the collar as she greeted her guest. By all the tail-wagging, it was obviously someone familiar—someone she trusted the mutt with since she didn't hesitate to release him.

But Amity seemed unsure about what to do next, taking a long look back at me before stepping across the threshold to join them on the porch.

Who was she out there with?

It sounded like a guy, but I couldn't hear anything but muted voices from where I was sitting, so I nudged the purring cat from my lap and went to the window.

Leaning past a brass floor lamp I could see long legs clad in blue jeans and rubber boots.

And the boots seemed to be very close to Amity's bare feet.

Were they embracing?

I pressed my cheek to the window to get a better view, but the boots took a step toward the house, disappearing from my field of vision.

Then the door creaked open.

Yikes!

I fingered the length of the Roman shade as if my "service" also included cleaning the curtains. "Well, hello again," I said as casually as I could to Killian while Amity shut the door behind him.

His face hardened much like it did yesterday morning. "Why are you back here?"

The smoky brown cat that had reclaimed the chair jumped down and skittered away as if I should follow its lead.

Yep, Smoky and I both knew that I'd been busted. "I—"

"I invited her," Amity said with an edge to her voice that suggested that she was in charge of this situation.

Settling between them, Max whimpered, clearly attuned to the rising tension in the room.

Killian sharpened his focus on me. "Why?"

Heaving a sigh, she pointed at the kitchen. "She's gonna clean up that mess."

Killian cocked his head as if he could see right through me. "No, she's not."

That felt like my cue to clear the air. "Actually..." I reached into my tote for the list of cleaning services I had intended to provide to Amity.

"I'll take care of it." He turned to his ex-wife as I approached, ignoring the sheet of paper in my hand. "Dad has some stuff in his shed that works great on floor tile." Killian's voice softened, as gentle as a caress. "I can get it now or I can come back later if you don't want to be here while..."

Lowering her gaze, she shook her head. "I don't want to go anywhere. I just want to get this done."

With a nod Killian stepped out the door, Max trotting behind him like a child who wanted to be with his dad.

Amity cursed. "Max, come!"

The scruffy mutt bounded back inside and was met by a big hug as he looked up at her adoringly, tail wagging. "Yes, you're a good boy and for that you get a cookie."

Max followed Amity to a wooden kitchen table with ornately carved legs, where a glass jar of dog biscuits sat next to a bowl of kiwis.

"Sorry if he was rude," she said, leaving Max to crunch alone in the dining area as if she couldn't stomach the proximity to her bloody kitchen. "Manners aren't Killian's best thing."

So I'd noticed.

"No worries. I know it's been rough." And I didn't want to make the situation any worse by making her think I was here on false pretenses, so I slipped the cleaning service printout back into my tote. "I should get going." Before Killian came back and accused me of wearing out my welcome. "But if there's anything I can do, don't hesitate to give me a call."

Because I'd love another chance to talk to you.

A guarded smile teased Amity's lips as she walked me to the door. "I think we've got it covered, but thanks."

The clean-up covered? Probably. But it felt like there was a lot going on here that had yet to be uncovered.

Chapter Seven

I spent the thirty-minute drive back to town trying to convince myself that there could be a rational explanation for everything I had witnessed at Amity's house.

Clearly, Amity and Killian still had some sort of bond. One that I sure didn't understand.

Because yesterday, I had seen for myself that Amity's hostility for her ex cut so deep that she had to be physically restrained. But this afternoon, she seemed to be as comfortable with him as an old pair of slippers.

I knew better than most that relationships could be complicated. But this was more than that.

This felt off.

The rage spewing from Amity after discovering her husband's body had been as genuine as the gut-wrenching tears I saw streaking down her face. And there was no mistaking it had been aimed at Killian.

I get the fact that our bodies can only burn red-hot for a short time before exhaustion sets in, but a righteous fire boiling your blood doesn't just snuff itself out after a good cry. Especially when the blood of the lost love you're grieving has yet to be scrubbed away. Specifi-

cally, by the hand of the man you were accusing of murder yesterday?

This made no sense.

Something had to have happened. Something big.
And since Carlos didn't act like he had any inside scoop
about it when he mentioned Amity staying at his place,
I'd wager that it happened shortly before I arrived.

But what?

I didn't have a clue, but I knew where I might be able
to find one. So, after a quick stop at Valu-Mart to pick up
the office supplies Patsy needed, I headed over to Duke's
to see if any breaking news had come across the gossip
circuit wires.

Knowing that it was in my best interest to maintain
that low profile Frankie expected of me, instead of parking out front on Main Street, I found a spot half a block
away and then slipped in through the diner's side door.

My great-aunt Alice looked up from the butcher block
worktable she had been wiping down. "Hi sweetie. Wait
a minute." She squinted at the clock mounted above an
antique red and white Coca Cola sign. "It isn't five yet.
Aren't you supposed to be working?"

"Yeah," Hector, Duke's longtime line cook, chimed in
from his post behind the grill. "You're not playing hooky,
are you, *mi querida*?"

There was no good answer I could provide without
getting into the reason I didn't want the pie happy hour
regulars in the dining room to see me. "No, I'm working.
At least I was. Frankie had a bunch of errands for me to
run and I finished early."

Hector gave me a knowing nod. "And you rushed over here because you can't get enough of my patty melts because they're so much better than the old man's."

"I heard that!" Duke bellowed from the counter, where he typically sat with a cup of decaf before handing over the reins to the night shift.

While Hector exchanged barbs with my great-uncle, Alice fixed her hazel eyes on me. "It's more like Frankie wanted to keep you away from the gossips you work with 'cause you're a witness to that Constantine kid's murder."

"Who told you that?"

"Jan stopped by for lunch, and of course, Lucille did her darndest to pump her for information."

Muttering a choice swear word, I crossed in front of the stainless steel refrigerator humming near her table and plopped my butt down on the closest stool.

"Of course." It was what the queen of Port Merritt's Gossip Central did best.

"You know how it goes around here."

All too well, but I resented being served up as the daily dish at my own family's restaurant.

Alice set her rag next to the fifty-pound sack of flour parked at the end of the table and took the stool across from me. "If it's any consolation, Jan didn't blab about anything that I didn't already know. Eleanor called last night and told me what happened."

It figured that Gram would want to share the big news with her sister, but that only shined a brighter light on my small role in this miserable story.

"So what do you think?" Alice asked, lowering her voice to a whisper as my cell phone started ringing. "Did Killian do it?"

Groaning, I reached into my tote to see who was calling me. "I have no idea." I also didn't recognize the number and muted my phone in case it was Jan's cousin wanting similar answers.

"But I thought you saw—"

"I saw him on the property, that's all."

"Which seems mighty suspicious, if you ask me."

True enough, but just because I saw him skulk around his ex-wife's house, that didn't mean he had anything to do with the murder.

"And him moving back home, right next door to his ex?" Alice shook her head. "That's downright fishy."

"Well, that does happen to be where his parents live, so—"

"He suddenly shows up not three months after the wedding. Don't even try to convince me that there's an explanation for this other than him wanting to make some sort of trouble."

That was as plausible an explanation as I'd been able to come up with over the course of the last day and a half.

Alice leaned closer. "I think it was some sort of last-ditch effort to get back together with his wife."

I stared across the table at her. "Seems like it would be smarter to do that *before* the wedding."

"From what I've heard around here, there's more money in it for the both of them now."

I knew she would have some juicy scuttlebutt. "What exactly have you heard?"

"You know that Trevor had decided to sell the business, right?"

"I heard something about that." Last night from Carlos.

"Well, Dorothy Constantine was in last Friday. You know, for breakfast with some of the ladies from the center."

I had waited enough tables here over the years to become familiar with most of the senior center regulars who would stop by after their exercise class, but I couldn't remember meeting a Dorothy. "Who's that, Trevor's mother?"

"Aunt. Married to Neil, who's worked at the farm supply for-flippin'-ever."

Him I knew from having gone there with Gram. "What did Dorothy have to say?"

Alice waited for the waitress scooping ice cream onto a slice of pie to return to the dining room before answering. "Not a lot. I think she was too ticked off by what Trevor did to the family to talk about it."

"What'd he do?"

"Left everything to his bride."

"Is that so shocking? I mean, Amity was his wife."

"She's also the one who convinced him to break off the negotiations with the family to sell to an outsider."

I squelched a gasp. "You mean like recently?"

"Dorothy made it sound like that decision had just happened. That they all found out about it at a family meeting last week."

"And once that sale happens, they could all be out of a job."

Alice nodded. "She doesn't know what they're gonna do. Neil's not ready to retire, and their son Spencer... I guess he was just spittin' mad at Trevor."

"Do you know if Trevor's wife was there for this meeting?" Because I didn't get a sense of any heated family drama from Amity.

"Dunno. But I'd bet dollars to doughnuts that she was the one behind it, and now look at her. She's going to be quite the wealthy woman once she finds the right buyer." Alice's gaze tightened behind her trifocals. "Kind of makes the timing of Killian hanging around next door all the more suspicious, don't you think?"

Yep, definitely. Especially after seeing them together today.

But I didn't want her to quote me on that. "Don't jump to any conclusions. It's still an open investigation."

Alice waved me off. "Well, if I were in charge of it, I'd be talking to Dorothy. I think she knows a lot more than she wanted to admit to."

Which made me think that it was high time for me to introduce myself to Dorothy Constantine.

Chapter Eight

"So what did you do today?" Steve asked as he washed his hands at my kitchen sink two hours later.

Absolutely nothing I felt compelled to admit to.

I kept my gaze on the basil I was sprinkling into a simmering pot of spaghetti sauce. "I had to go to Seattle to deliver a subpoena, so I spent half the day waiting in line for a ferry."

"You get all the fun assignments."

"Nobody threw anything at me this time. Sort of sucks the fun out of being the delivery girl when I need to duck."

Steve stepped up behind me and nuzzled my neck. "I would never consider throwing anything at you if you showed up unannounced at my workplace."

I patted his hand. "How sweet. Of course, you work in a secured building, so it's not like I can just show up."

"Since when does that stop you when you want something?"

"Hey, it's usually with food, but if you don't want me to provide the occasional delivery from Duke's, tell Wanda to stop buzzing me in."

"Right. And inform the Chief and his secretary that I'm cutting off our supply of free apple fritters? I don't think so."

My black bear of a dog pushed his snout between us as if to tell us to stop snuggling and hurry up with the food that he hoped we'd soon share.

"I see you've also trained your dog to show up uninvited."

I reached past Steve for the box of angel hair pasta on the tile counter. "I like to think of it as a natural talent."

"Uh-huh." Pointing at the table I'd set in the adjoining dining room, he looked at the chow/lab mix at his feet. "Then he should also know when three's a crowd and go lie down."

Whimpering, Fozzie slipped me a mournful glance as if he wanted Mom to belay that order.

"Nice try, but you heard him," I said, stirring a handful of the pasta into boiling water. "Out of the kitchen."

Huffing his displeasure at his banishment, Fozzie sauntered just past the refrigerator and then lowered his belly to the hardwood floor.

I smiled over my shoulder at my fur ball. "Good boy. Well, good enough since you're still technically in the kitchen. Looks like he thought he needed to park close enough to keep an eye on you."

"That reminds me." Leaning against the counter, Steve folded his arms across his chest. "I was driving past the senior center on my way back to the station and saw your car parked out front."

"Yeah?" I stifled a cringe as the cell phone charging

next to the refrigerator rang, displaying the same number as earlier. "Fancy that."

"You need to get that?" he asked.

And talk to a reporter right in front of him?

I sent the call to voice mail. "No."

"Okay. So tell me, what were you doing at the senior center?"

Returning to the stove, I gave the pasta a stir. "Nothing."

"Then why were you parked there?"

"Sheesh, you're so suspicious. You should be a cop."

"And you're being evasive."

"Don't be ridiculous." I aimed my wooden spoon at the bottle of wine I picked up on my way home. "Why don't you make yourself useful and open that."

"Like I said, evasive." Steve smirked. "What is it you don't want me to know?"

"Nothing. Because I didn't go to the senior center. I went to Duke's and picked up a slice of pie for us to share for dessert." Which happened to be conveniently true.

"Parked kind of far away, didn't you?"

"Is that suddenly a crime?"

"Nope."

I hoped that would bring an end to this conversation. "Now that we've settled that, how about opening that wine?"

"It just struck me as unusual, especially for that time of day," Steve said, rummaging through the wrong utensil drawer for the corkscrew. "You know, when you should be working."

I pushed him aside, grabbed the corkscrew from the next drawer down, and slapped it onto the counter. "If you must know, Frankie didn't need me in the office today, so I knocked off a little early and went to pie happy hour."

"Uh-huh."

"What's that supposed to mean?"

"Just that it's interesting that you decided you needed some pie today of all days."

"Excuse me for thinking about what you'd like for dessert."

The corners of Steve's lips curled into a humorless smile. "So what did you find out?"

I hated that he could read me that easily. "You mean about the murder?"

"I'm sure Lucille has a theory about who did it. She always does."

"If she does, I don't know anything about it. The only person I talked to was Alice, and that was just for a few minutes."

"Yeah. To download every bit of gossip she had," Steve retorted as he uncorked the bottle of zinfandel.

"It wasn't like that." It couldn't be if I wanted to enjoy sharing that wine with him over the next couple of hours. "Everyone's just trying to make sense out of how Trevor Constantine could have been murdered."

"You should know by now that these things don't always make sense." He turned to me after popping the cork. "No matter how much we may want them to."

That felt like a warning. "You have to admit it's strange, though—how he was killed right after deciding to sell the family business."

Pouring two glasses, Steve grimaced. "And how would you happen to know that?"

"People like to talk to me."

"Right. And you would be advised not to repeat any of that talk because you shouldn't be getting more involved in this case than you already are."

"It's still strange. I mean the timing can't just be a coincidence, can it?"

He turned that grimace on me. "I wouldn't know. It's not my case, and I have no opinion on the matter."

I didn't need to search his face to know that last part was a big fat lie. "Sure."

"Is dinner almost ready? I'm starving," Steve said, stepping over Fozzie to carry our wineglasses to the dining room.

That was an evasive maneuver if ever I'd seen one.

Steve definitely knew something. Something that he clearly had no intention of sharing with me.

Darn it!

✳

When I arrived at my desk the next morning and checked my messages, I found that I had missed five calls: one a recording in Chinese that sounded as if I had won something, which I promptly deleted. Then one from Jan's cousin Linda that was almost word for word the same as the voice message she'd left on my cell phone last night—that she had a few quick questions for me.

I didn't care how quick they were. My name could not appear in the local paper. "I'd like to keep this job, thank you very much," I said, pressing delete.

Next was an apology from Jan for all the calls from her cousin. If she felt that badly about siccing Linda on me, I wished she'd tell her cousin to back off. Because not only was she calling my cell again, there were two more voice messages from her, pleading with me to call before the noon deadline she was up against.

"Not gonna happen." I pushed away from my desk with the satisfaction that her story would have to get written without me if she wanted it to hit the front page of tomorrow's *Gazette*.

I now needed to turn my focus on what to do with the more important story Alice had told me about the growing friction within the Constantine family. Which was little more than juicy gossip, but if everything that Dorothy had confided in Alice was true, shouldn't the detective in charge of the investigation be informed about it?

"Preferably by a family member who was actually there," I muttered as I entered the breakroom to pour myself a cup of the coffee I had set to brew ten minutes earlier.

Shondra looked up from the creamer she was stirring into her coffee cup. "Is your morning starting off so bad that you're talkin' to yourself, Charmaine?"

Yes, and I wasn't thrilled that she had overheard me. At the same time I knew that an opportunity had just dropped into my lap.

"I'm sort of working through a decision I have to make." Keeping my voice low in case anyone else came into the room, I joined her in front of the coffeemaker. "Because I came into some information that might be relevant to Detective Pearson's investigation."

Her jaw tightened. "Why on God's green earth are you the one coming into *any* information?"

I forced a smile. "It was sort of a right place, right time thing."

"I bet. And when exactly did this happen?"

"Yesterday afternoon."

Shondra blew out a coffee-scented breath. "In other words, after you'd been instructed not to discuss the case with anyone."

"I didn't. At least that hadn't been my intention." Because I wanted Alice to do all the talking. "Someone came to me with some background information that I'd sure want to know about if I was the one in charge of the investigation."

Turning away from me so that I couldn't read her face, Shondra dropped her stir stick into the trash. "And who might that be?" she asked in the tart tone I'd heard her use on hostile witnesses.

I wanted to keep Alice's name out of this. "A family member."

"A member of Trevor Constantine's family?"

"A member of my family."

"*Your* family!" She stepped toward me, her dark eyes hard as glass. "Oh, don't tell me. Let me guess. This information came from Duke's."

I tried to think of a way to phrase it so that it wouldn't sound like run of the mill gossip. "Um…"

"In other words you want to pass along some gossip."

Crap. There was no denying it. "But it came from a reliable source."

"Then let the source go to Detective Pearson, 'cause I guarantee that he's not gonna want to hear any third-hand information from you."

"What if she doesn't want to go to the police?" I asked, trying to keep up with Shondra as she stalked toward the door.

"You're pretty good with people. Even though you can be a real pain in the butt sometimes."

Gee, thanks.

"Be persuasive."

"Right." That sounded a lot easier said than done.

Shondra looked back over her shoulder. "Other than that, remember that you're a witness and stay the heck out of this."

Also easier said than done.

Chapter Nine

Almost three hours later, I stood next to my great-aunt Alice's bubbling fish tank and hoped that I had arrived in time to find Dorothy Constantine lingering over a cup of Duke's bad coffee.

"You're taking an early lunch." Lucille, Duke's longest-tenured waitress and chief gossipmonger, closed in on me in her squeaky orthopedic shoes as if I were the special of the day. "Is something goin' on, or are you just back to ask more questions about—"

"Shhh!" Since we were turning most of the heads near the door, I couldn't afford to have her finish that sentence. "Come with me," I said, making a beeline for the kitchen.

Duke pointed his spatula at me through the cutout window. "Shouldn't you be working right about now?" He scowled at Lucille. "Like some other people around here?"

She waved him off. "I'm takin' a break."

"Your break was when you sat down with those cackling biddies in the corner," he grumbled as they erupted in laughter.

Good. The Gray Ladies, as the seniors from that exercise class called themselves, were still here.

"Then I'm takin' another one!" Lucille declared, pushing open the swinging door. "Char and I need a little privacy to confer about important matters, so back off."

Egads. Subtlety had never been Lucille's strong suit, but I really needed her to get a clue before someone I worked with came in and overheard us.

I also didn't need any trouble from Duke, who was leveling an angry glare on me like a heat-seeking missile. "Then she had better make this conference snappy if she knows what's good for her."

No kidding.

I smiled sweetly at the curmudgeon with the silver crew cut. "This'll only take a second." Because as soon as Lucille pointed out Dorothy, I intended to find us a quiet table for two.

"Like heck it will." Lucille leaned into me, her light blue eyes wide with anticipation. "What gives? Something juicy?"

"Nope." I tried to act casual. Anything less and she'd make it her mission to squeeze me dry. "Nothing like that."

"Then what's goin' on?"

I took her by the arm and angled behind Duke, using his six-foot-three frame like a human shield from the ladies in the corner.

"Hey!" he protested while turning the three sizzling strips of bacon that were making my mouth water. "What do you think you're doing back there?"

I patted his back. "You don't want to know." Because he'd probably rat me out to Steve.

Cursing under his breath, my great-uncle shook his head. "I was afraid you were going to say that."

"Never mind him. I wanna know." Lucille rose to her tiptoes to look over his shoulder. "Is someone out there?"

That was what I wanted to find out.

"Ooh, I know!" she proclaimed with enough volume to raise the bushy eyebrows of the lone trucker at the counter. "It's someone else you want to question. Who is it? Another suspect?"

Good grief, Lucille! "Shhh!! I told you, it's not like that."

"I knew that Killian kid didn't do it." She nudged Duke out of the way to get an unobstructed view out of the window. "But I can't imagine that anyone here would've wanted to bump off Trevor."

Duke groaned. "That's enough. Out. Both of you."

"Just a second." I leaned close to whisper in Lucille's ear. "Is Dorothy Constantine out there?"

She wheeled around, her brow a roadmap of wrinkles. "You can't possibly think she's a suspect."

"Charmaine," Duke growled, wielding his spatula like a flyswatter. "What did I just say?"

"We were just leaving." I pushed Lucille toward the door before I came away with a big grease stain on my khakis.

"What's all the commotion about?" Alice asked, crossing the kitchen with a berry pie in her hands. Instead of waiting for an answer, she narrowed her eyes at me. "And why aren't you at work?"

After everything she confided in me yesterday, did I really have to explain why I was back? "I took an early lunch."

Lucille jabbed her thumb in my direction. "She's here because she thinks Dorothy's involved in the murder."

No, no, no. "You said that, not me. I just want to talk to her." I gave Alice a nod. "You know, to follow up on a couple things." *That you told me yesterday.*

My great-aunt's cheeks flushed. "Oh. Well, I'm sure there's no harm in that. Seeing that's part of your job and all."

Don't mention Alice's name. Message received loud and clear.

I cracked open the kitchen door to see if the head count of the ladies at the corner table had changed. "Is she sitting out there?"

"No, and order up!" Duke barked.

Lucille rolled her eyes. "Sorry, hon. You just missed her."

"Crap." While Lucille squeaked away with someone's brunch order, I turned to Alice. "I obviously didn't take an early enough lunch."

"Don't be so sure about that." Lowering her voice, she cocked her head. "In fact, why don't you step into my office."

I followed her back to her worktable. "What do you know?"

"Dorothy had her usual Tuesday to-go order with her

when she left. So I know where you can find her if you hurry."

Great. "Where?"

"At the farm supply store. Been having lunch there with Neil Tuesdays and Thursdays ever since she retired."

Then I hoped they'd be agreeable to me joining them.

"But none of this came from me," Alice added with a shake of her head.

"No problem. As far as anyone there will know, I'll just be there to shop on my lunch hour."

She scoffed. "For what? A tractor?"

"I'm sure I can find something I can use." Preferably, some answers.

After ten minutes of scouring the store's shelves, I had yet to find anything cheap that I could use. Worse, Neil and his wife were nowhere in sight. Not in the main building where the youngest Constantine I had seen Sunday was helping a customer in denim overalls at the counter, and not in the red storage barn set back in the middle of the property.

Running into Dorothy here was feeling less likely by the second, and with a half-hour drive back to the courthouse, I had no more time to waste.

Fortunately, with the guy in the overalls heading for the door, the Constantine behind the counter turned his attention to me. Unfortunately, his face turned to stone when we locked eyes.

Yep, he knew exactly where he had seen me last.

"Can I help you find something?" he asked using the surly tone Duke reserves for salesmen and glad-handing politicians.

"I sure hope so." Smiling to lighten the mood, I zeroed in on the name badge above the breast pocket of his plaid shirt as I approached the counter. "Hi, Spencer. Is Dorothy around?"

His heavy brows furrowed, tugging on the bruise outlining his left eye like a yellowing half moon. "Why?"

An honest answer to that question was going to get me nowhere. Not with this guy acting like a sentry guarding the family castle.

"My grandmother and I were here Sunday." I rolled my eyes for effect. "What am I saying? Of course, you know that. It just got so crazy that afternoon, and ... well, I was in the area to pick up some ..." I looked behind him at several plastic sacks of chicken manure stacked against the wall. "Some fertilizer for my raised beds and thought I should take the opportunity to offer our condolences."

His stubble-covered jaw unclenched but his brown eyes remained guarded. "I'll pass that along."

It looked like a dishonest answer was also going to get me nowhere.

"How are you doing?" I asked to see if I could chip away at the wall of ice Spencer had erected between us.

The smirk teasing the corner of his mouth told me I was wasting my time. "Great."

I pointed at his bruise. "Looks like that would hurt."

"It's nothing."

Since he had a greenish bruise on the back of his right hand, it was an easy guess that he'd been in a fight. Fairly recently, too.

I leaned in to shoot him a flirtatious smile. "I expected you to say that I should have seen the other guy."

Spencer broke eye contact and blanched as if a portion of that ice wall had penetrated his skin.

A fight that it looked like he wasn't proud of.

Did tempers flare so hot at that family meeting that he came to blows with his cousin Trevor?

"I'm sorry. I shouldn't have said that," I intoned with a liberal dollop of sincerity while I watched for a reaction. "I heard that you and Trevor had words."

Spencer stepped back from the counter, effectively signaling the end of this conversation, but not before regret consumed all trace of that smirk.

"You know how people talk." I dangled the suggestion in front of him like bait on a hook. If he wanted to set me and Gossip Central straight, now was his opportunity.

Instead he blew out a breath. "So what are you growing?"

Huh? "Growing?"

"You said you had raised beds."

Oh yeah. "Mainly flowers." Because of the bulbs that Barry had planted under the picture window. "And tomatoes." Since Gram had insisted that I take home one of the five plants she bought Sunday.

"Tomatoes love chicken manure. You just want to be careful how much you use." Spencer slanted me a glance as he reached for the smallest of the bags behind him. "It's not good to spread it on too thick."

I had a sinking feeling that he wasn't referring only to the chicken poop. "Got it. That should be all I need then." Truly, because I could take a hint.

As he rang up my purchase, his face seemed to relax and I wondered if I had heard a warning when all this guy had provided was some good gardening advice.

"Hope it works out for you," Spencer said, handing me the bag.

"I'm sure it will. I'll just be careful not to use too much."

His lips twisted into a chilling smile. "Yeah, you be careful."

My sinking feeling dropped to the pit of my stomach. Because there was no mistaking that I had just been warned.

Chapter Ten

Steve had called about a case that was going to keep him busy for a couple of hours, so after I got home and fed Fozzie, I headed out for groceries. I needed chicken for the cacciatore I had planned for dinner, and all I had on hand was a whole lot of chicken poop.

That I was never going to use.

That gave me the creeps when I thought about the guy who sold it to me.

And it was stinking up the cargo hold of my Subaru.

"It has to go," I said, taking a detour down G Street, where my grandmother's Victorian was perched on a large corner lot.

"I have a little gift for you," I told Gram moments later, when I found her watering the row of tomato plants bordering her patio.

Setting down her watering can, she squinted at the five-pound bag I was holding at arm's length. "Chicken manure?"

"Yeah, I saw it at the store and thought of you."

"How very touching." She pointed at the umbrella-covered table behind me. "Why don't you set it down since you're obviously trying to unload it."

"I wouldn't put it quite that way." Although she was absolutely right. "You have all these tomato plants and tomatoes love chicken manure, so..."

"You've had a tomato plant for three days and now you're an expert on what to feed them?"

"Hardly. That's what Spencer at the farm supply store told me, so I thought—"

"You went back there?"

I nodded.

"Why?" she demanded, the puckers surrounding her mouth echoing her disapproval. "And don't even pretend that it was for fertilizer."

"I heard something about a Constantine family meeting that got a little heated—"

"From Lucille, no doubt."

"It doesn't matter who I heard it from." Especially since Alice wouldn't appreciate me ratting her out to her older sister. "I was just hoping to encourage someone to go to the sheriff's department about it."

Gram sucked in a breath. "Because that's what set off that fight between Trevor and Killian?"

It sounded like she'd heard some juicy gossip that had yet to make it to Gossip Central. "What fight?"

"Well, *fight* might be overstating it. Gaylene made it sound more like a shouting match."

"When did this happen?"

"When we went back to the tea room, a few minutes before Steve showed up to drive me home."

"No, I meant what day did they have this shouting

match?"

"Oh." Gram shrugged. "I don't know. Killian only moved back home a couple of weeks ago, so it had to have been pretty recently."

I dropped into the closest of the four chairs surrounding the table. "True." But how recently? And did their war of words lead to the events of Sunday?

"Gaylene didn't want to believe that her son could have had anything to do with the murder," Gram added, giving voice to what I'd been thinking as she took a seat next to me. "The boys had been so tight, ever since high school. But given how that relationship fell apart—"

"With Trevor hooking up with his ex."

"I guess."

What? "You think there was something else going on between them?"

I got another shrug. "I don't know any specifics beyond what Gaylene told me."

"Which was?"

"That she knew Amity would be trouble from the first moment she met her."

From everything I'd seen and heard since Sunday, it seemed that Mrs. Havens had been right about her former daughter-in-law.

"And what does that girl do? She practically rubs the Havenses' noses in her husband *upgrade* by living next door. And now that boy's dead." Gram's shoulders slumped as if they couldn't support the weight of her words. "And Killian's the prime suspect."

I didn't know how to respond to Gram's "husband

upgrade" comment. Neither one of us could crawl inside Amity's head to understand her motivations. But one thing seemed clear: Amity Havens Constantine had been the instigator behind some of the multi-family drama that had been brewing since the day she came to town.

Yep, she'd proven herself to be trouble.

But did she bear any responsibility for her second husband's death?

My gut told me maybe.

It also told me that I needed to be very, very careful the next time I spoke to her.

✳

"That was great," Steve said two hours later, after mopping up the last of the sauce on his plate with a slice of garlic bread.

It was such an innocuous statement—a common nicety exchanged between couples after sharing a meal. But it made me envision the other couple that had been on my mind most of the day, and I wondered how Trevor and Amity had spent their last evening together.

Had it been a Saturday date night that ended in one another's arms?

Or had Amity snuck over to the berry field to see Killian and that was what prompted that shouting match?

Again, my gut wanted to weigh in with a definite maybe, but…

"So is it pie for dessert again?" Steve asked, calling a

time-out to my musing, but with a tone that didn't sound quite so innocuous.

The dog at my feet snapped to attention at the mention of dessert, which probably indicated that I had indulged in letting him lick too many ice cream bowls. "Nope, sorry to disappoint."

"Too bad. You didn't have the compulsion to go to pie happy hour today, huh?"

"No." I scooted my chair back to collect our plates. "And I resent your insinuation."

"That's not insinuation." The candle between us added a warm glow to the flicker of amusement in Steve's eyes. "I know you."

"You know nothing." And given where I'd been today I preferred that it stay that way.

He picked up our empty wineglasses and followed me to the kitchen with Fozzie hot on his heels. "I know that you don't go to Duke's for the pie."

"You're right. I go to visit my family. The occasional piece of pie I come home with is just a side benefit. For *you*, I might add."

"I see. Then where's my pie?"

Fozzie barked as if Steve needed some backup, and I opened the dishwasher door to distance myself from their annoyingly frequent male alliance. "For a detective who's usually pretty good with details, you don't seem to be paying attention. I didn't go to pie happy hour."

"I know. You were there earlier, but apparently not for the food."

Was Lucille incapable of keeping her mouth shut? "I

may have stopped by while I was out running errands."

"To visit your family," Steve stated, transferring the wineglasses to the top rack of the dishwasher while Fozzie settled at his feet. "Because there's really no other reason for you to just stop by, right?"

"That insinuation seems to have snuck back into your tone, and I have to say that I don't much care for it."

Shutting the dishwasher, he wrapped his arms around my waist. "That sounds like a guilty conscience talking."

"I'm sure I don't know what you mean."

He pulled me close. "You know exactly what I mean, and I'd like you to back off."

Clasping my hands behind his neck, I flattened my breasts against his chest. "Back off?"

"Well, maybe not this very minute."

"Why? Did you have something in mind?"

Steve's lips curved as he lowered his mouth to mine. "Seeing as there's no pie, maybe we could do something else for dessert."

"Mmmm. Maybe we could."

Chapter Eleven

I spent most of Wednesday morning as a jury consultant to assistant prosecutor Lisa Arbuckle in Judge Witten's courtroom.

At least that's how I was introduced to the court. The extent of my "consulting" consisted of passing a note to Lisa when I spotted bias bubbling to the surface in a prospective juror. Other than that I was expected to only speak when spoken to, wear a suit, and hustle back to make a fresh pot of coffee every time we had a break.

Fine.

That was a small price to pay for a seat at the long mahogany table across from the defendant and her attorney. Especially for this case, because it involved a middle-aged office manager Steve had arrested last May for embezzling over two hundred thousand dollars from the biggest construction company in town.

I didn't know the woman. Nor did I recognize the name Barbara DeMatteo, but something about the intensity behind her dark blue eyes when she passed by my table at recess felt oddly familiar.

Out of curiosity, when I got back to my desk, I ran a

background check on Barbara that made her look squeaky clean—a good hire for a trusted office position, aside from the pesky matter of a felony embezzlement indictment. But it wasn't until I did an internet search and her name came up on an old Port Townsend newspaper obituary that I discovered the reason why Barbara DeMatteo looked familiar.

Listed among the other surviving family members of Barbara's late mother were three grandchildren—one named Brooke.

Apply some dewy foundation to freshen that fifty-year-old face, then darken her bob to a rich brunette, and Barbara could pass as the twin of the Brooke I waited on Sunday.

Mystery solved. And as a bonus this gave me a probable last name for Brooke, which I promptly typed in the search bar.

As I'd expected for a pretty twenty-something, the first of the hundred plus results was a link to a popular social media website. Within two seconds I found several pictures of Brooke and Joel.

Bingo.

Scrolling through her photos it didn't take me long to find a haunting image of Trevor with Amity. Also one with Brooke and Amity dressed as big-haired zombies for Halloween, puckering their matching black lips to ham it up for the camera. But that was it for photos that included Amity. Which seemed odd for gal pals who had clearly collaborated on their Halloween costumes.

Did the girls have a falling-out?

I popped over to Amity Constantine's account to see if there was anything there that could help me answer that question.

Nope. Just a few cat and dog photos to accompany what looked to be a professional image of Amity saying "I do" to Trevor. But that was it. No pictures of Brooke. Nothing in a post to indicate that they had ever been friends. Which made me wonder if Amity could use one.

✳

"Surprise!" Marietta squealed six hours later, extending her arms to greet me when I stepped through my grandmother's back door.

"Hello." While my mother enveloped me in a jasmine-infused embrace, I looked to Gram to clue me in. "Is there something going on that I should know about?" Because the only reason Marietta ever crashed our Wednesday dinner get-togethers was when she wanted something.

"Not that I've been informed of." Gram glanced up from the head of lettuce she'd been chopping with a vengeance. "Yet."

My mother gave my arm a playful swat. "Oh, you two. Can't I join my two favorite girls for a simple meal?"

She wanted something, all right. I knew it couldn't have anything to do with the story on the front page of today's *Gazette* because there had been no mention of anyone she would know.

"Are you here by yourself?" I asked. "Where's Barry?"

"He has a teacher's meeting, so it's just us girls until he picks me up in a couple of hours." Marietta returned to the kitchen table where she had been sitting with a glass of white wine and motioned for me to take the seat next to her. "Unless of course, Steve will be joining us."

She knew very well that Steve and I had this standing dinner date with her mother. "Yes, he'll be joining us." Although I didn't see his pickup in his driveway when I pulled up. "He's probably just working late."

"Which is fine," Gram chimed in. "The potatoes won't be done for a few minutes yet."

Marietta's raspberry red lips curled with satisfaction. "That gives us a little time to chat then."

Uh-oh. "What about?"

With a sigh she reached for her wineglass. "You needn't sound so underwhelmed to spend some time with your mother. I've hardly seen you for weeks."

Excuse me? "I saw you on Mother's Day."

"For five minutes."

Now it was my turn to sigh. "As you'll recall, some other things were going on that took up my time."

"Yes, yes. But I didn't get a chance to talk to you about something before you rushed off."

Oh please, don't let this have anything to do with sex, getting married again, or the mother/daughter spa day I had promised her last Christmas.

Her emerald eyes brightened. "As you know, Barry's birthday is coming up."

I stifled a cringe while Gram delivered another glass of wine to the table.

"Oh goody," she chirped with false cheer, giving me the *look* to play nice.

The last thing I had time for this week was planning a birthday party. "Yeah, goody."

Marietta sniffed the air. "Mama, is the roast burning?"

Gram hadn't once burned a pot roast in the thirty-two years since I'd come to live with her, and we all knew it.

She heaved a sigh before retreating to the kitchen. "I can take a hint."

"It's just that I want to talk to Charmaine about something," Marietta called after her and then shot me a conspiratorial grin. "Because I want it to be a surprise."

She wanted me to throw him a surprise party? Even worse. "Mom—"

"Oh, don't even say it. I know he won't want us to make a fuss. He's just not that kind of guy."

Then what was she talking about?

"But I saw something I think he'd like." She pulled her smartphone from the sparkly clutch that coordinated with her jeweled lace blouse. "I took a picture."

I stared at the blurry image she'd pulled up on her phone. "Who's that?"

"My next-door neighbor."

"Okay." Holding it closer, I could make out the lilac bush in bloom at the corner of the property line they shared. "What exactly am I supposed to be looking at?"

She pointed at the lawnmower the size of a combine the old dude was riding. "That."

"Whoa. It's huge."

"What is? Let me see." Gram leaned over my shoulder and took the phone from my hand. "Well, this is a horrible picture. I can barely make out that it's Arthur."

Marietta snatched back her phone. "Never mind that. What do you think about getting a riding lawnmower like that for Barry?"

He had bequeathed me his push mower and upgraded to a cordless electric one last year when I rented his old house. "I don't know that he particularly needs it."

She tittered as if I had said something adorable. "Sweetie, presents aren't necessarily about what we need, now are they?"

I had a feeling that was a reference to that spa day I was supposed to have arranged and kept my mouth shut.

"Mary Jo," Gram said, easing onto the hardback chair across from her daughter. "I'm sure Arthur has that riding lawnmower because of his bad knees, not because he has rolling hills of grass to cut."

Marietta dropped the smile. "Maybe all the years of pushing heavy equipment around gave him those bad knees. Did you ever think of that?"

"Heavy equipment," Gram scoffed. "What I think is that all the years you spent in Hollywood gave you a flair for the dramatic."

"Okay, that might have been a teensy exaggeration, but we do have a yard with a lot of grass and I thought it could be fun for Barry to cut it in style." My mother stared wistfully at the image on her phone. "Maybe on some sort of tractor thingee that's not quite this big. They make those, right?"

Tractor thingees? "I'm sure they do."

Actually, I knew for a fact that they came in all shapes and sizes because I'd seen a barn full of tractors at Constantine Farm Supply. Riding lawnmowers, too.

Marietta tapped her phone to open a search engine. "Where would you look for such a thing?"

"Not online," I said, trying to sound as cool and neutral as vanilla ice cream about the opportunity unfolding before me. "Because there's a place right outside of town that should have exactly what you're looking for."

My mother beamed. "Fantastic! Could we go?"

If you insist.

"I don't have any plans for Saturday, so you betcha." I'd be willing to make a full mother/daughter day of it if it would give me another Constantine family member to chat with.

"Wait a minute." Gram leaned in. "You're not suggesting going back to the scene of the crime, are you?"

"Crime." Marietta pressed a manicured hand to the base of her throat. "You mean that murder?"

"It didn't happen anywhere near where we'd be." Not super near, anyway. "And if we get there before two, we could have lunch at the tea room next door since you missed out last Sunday."

"Ooh, I'd love that. In fact, Mama, you should come too. It would be like a Mother's Day do-over."

Gram shot me a wary glance. "I don't know. Are you sure this is a good idea so soon after you-know-what happened?"

Oh, yes. A Mother's Day do-over was the best idea I'd

had all week. We would just skip the murder part of the do-over.

Chapter Twelve

"Okay. What was going on with your mother?" Steve asked the instant the front door shut behind Marietta and Barry. "She smiled at you all through dinner."

"Breaking news. She kinda likes me." I linked my arm with his to lead him back to the kitchen, where tonight's dirty dishes awaited us. "I am her daughter, after all."

"Yeah, but that's not why she showed up tonight."

"You know how bored she can get when she's not working. She probably just wanted to get out of the house and think about something else."

"Oh, she was thinking about something else, all right." He pulled me closer. "So what's going on Saturday?"

I'd had a sinking feeling that Marietta asking about the weather forecast for Saturday might lead to this moment. "I'm taking her shopping."

"You hate shopping with your mother. What'd she do? Guilt you into it?"

"Nope." Although she was highly skilled in that regard. "We're sort of having a Mother's Day do-over since she got the short end of the stick last Sunday." Grabbing the towel I had set out to dry the dishes, I hoped that served as a sufficiently plausible explanation because I really didn't want to lie to the man I loved.

"Sounds like guilt to me."

"That's because you have a suspicious mind."

"Which is what you always say when you don't want me to know what you're up to."

My heart skipped a beat. "Don't be ridiculous."

"Uh-huh. You say that too."

I clearly needed to acquire a fresh set of comebacks. "Okay, then how about this. If you think my mother and I are scheming about something, you can come with us."

"I'm sure I'm busy Saturday."

As I'd expected he'd say. "Oh? Doing what?"

"I'll find something to do."

I draped the towel around his neck and pulled him close for a kiss. "Coward."

"To spend the day shopping with your mother? You got that right. You can have all that fun without me."

I didn't anticipate having any fun at all. But if an afternoon with Marietta helped to solve a murder, it would be well worth every minute.

✳

I woke up in a cold sweat around two, my heart pounding from dreaming that my mother was trying to cut me down with a giant lawnmower.

"What the heck?" Did my subconscious want me to believe that Marietta enjoyed tormenting me?

"No way," I whispered to the dog snoring at the foot of my bed.

It only felt that way sometimes.

And it was just a stupid dream.

I stared at the ceiling, reminding myself that there was nothing about our plan for Saturday to worry about. As long as she didn't do any of the test-driving and I was careful about what I said—to my mother and every Constantine family member we'd soon encounter.

After watching the sun rise over the bay during a jog down to the park with Fozzie, I took a long, hot shower and felt almost convinced that everything would be okay. Today, for round two of jury selection, as well as on Saturday.

I just needed to get rid of the fuzzy ache behind my eyes to be totally convinced.

With the aid of three aspirin, a pot of Italian roast, and the energy drink I bought on my way to work, my body was humming with more buzz than fuzz by the time the bailiff called our session to order at nine-ten. But that buzz vacated the premises an hour later, and by eleven I really needed to pee.

Mercifully, no one raised an objection to Luther Purdy, a likeable senior I knew from Duke's Cafe, who was seated as our twelfth and final juror.

And that was that.

I was minutes away from being excused from court. Yay and amen.

Part of me wished I could sneak in after lunch to hear the opening arguments because I didn't know any more about the deep doo-doo Barbara DeMatteo found herself in than I did yesterday. Beyond what I could observe, anyway.

And based on appearances, did I think she was guilty?

The ashen woman in black Chanel who looked like she had dressed for her own funeral?

Yep, and I would have re-thought the pricey suit.

But none of that mattered, especially in that moment because I really, really needed to pee.

"Do you need anything else from me?" I asked Lisa after Judge Witten adjourned the session with the rap of his gavel. *Please say no.*

With her legal assistant approaching our table Lisa waved me away, and I dashed out of the courtroom like Fozzie let off his leash.

"Char," Jan called after me as I bolted past the reception desk. "A few of us are going to the Roadkill Grill for lunch. Want to join us?"

"Thanks, but I already have plans." And they didn't include me becoming the one they grilled for a play-by-play of everything I had witnessed at the murder scene.

The only place I wanted to go for my lunch hour was home for a power nap. So after making a quick pit stop, I grabbed my tote and headed for the door.

Hearing voices from the top of the stairs, I looked over to see Barbara DeMatteo and her attorney in a huddle on the wooden bench opposite the courtroom we had just exited.

Since this lunch break was also one of the few opportunities for family members to have physical contact with their loved one standing trial, I made a quick scan of the gold and black tiled landing to see who had turned out to show their support for Barbara.

No one.

No Brooke, no sons who had been mentioned in that obituary, no husband.

Just Barbara muttering something while she stared down at her black pumps, and the defense attorney who was probably charging a bundle to pat her hand. Almost like a friend offering her condolences at a funeral—the one that Barbara had overdressed for.

Which struck me as incredibly sad.

But only for a second because the sheriff's deputy standing guard between the two courtrooms gave me the pointed stare I get from Duke when I overstay my welcome in his kitchen.

Got it.

Move on. Nothing to see here.

Absolutely right. Also not another family drama that I wanted to get sucked into.

"What you need to focus on right now is getting some sleep," I reminded myself when I settled behind the wheel of my car.

That's when my stomach rumbled as if to suggest that I had better quiet it down before my head hit the pillow. Fortunately, there was a little market three blocks up from Broward Park that featured a deli with ready-made sandwiches.

I'd discovered it shortly after I moved in because it was

just past the day spa where I had once taken Marietta to get her acrylic nails repaired.

The spa we were supposed to return to for our mother/daughter treatment day.

And as I drove past it, the spa that appeared to have received its own renovation treatment with a new, upscale façade. A new name too—*Le Calme, a Boutique Day Spa.*

"Wow." The converted Craftsman that had been a dog grooming salon back when I was a kid, was now modern and trendy-looking.

Good for them. But not so good for me because Marietta would want that spa day all the more once she caught a glimpse of the canvas "Coming soon" sign attached to the azure awning over the door.

The door that Brooke DeMatteo was opening.

Which explained why I didn't see her at the courthouse, but what the heck did she have to do with this spa?

Pulling into the market's lot, I parked in the first spot I could find and scrambled out of the car while keeping Brooke in my peripheral vision.

I made a point of glancing in her direction as she walked by. "Well, hello again," I said with a friendly wave.

Brooke stopped and squinted at me, shielding her eyes against the glare of the overhead sun. "Hi." Her glossy lips stretched into a polite smile. "Sorry, I know we've met before, but…"

"Sunday at Eddie's. I waited on your table."

"Right." She dropped the smile. "Nice to see you again." She turned and started for the market. Clearly, Brooke was in no mood to get chatty with the *help*.

Since we shared a destination, I didn't hesitate to follow her. That was when I noticed the overhead sun highlighting so many streaks of sage green paint in her hair that she looked like a walking herb garden. "Hold up."

Brooke stepped into the broad shadow of the market and huffed her displeasure at me. "I'm sorry. I don't have a lot of time."

No, you just don't want to make time for me.

I didn't care. I wasn't going to let this chance to chat slip away from me and gently picked out two blobs of paint from the crown of her head. "There." I held them out to her as proof positive that she could trust me, at least for the next few minutes. "That was the worst of it. The rest is barely noticeable until you get up close."

Wincing, she glanced down at her paint-splattered jeans and sneakers. "Thanks. The way it's been going today, I think I've got more paint on me than the walls."

"Are you working on the spa next door?" As if I didn't know. "When I drove by I noticed it's under renovation."

"Oh, this is much more than a renovation project." Brooke's creamy cheeks puffed with pride. "It's being transformed into a beauty and wellness oasis. Within a year I fully expect that we'll be *the* premier day spa destination on the peninsula."

Wow. This chick sounded like she was quoting the ad scheduled to promote the place, but the passion lighting her eyes was what convinced me that she was a true believer.

Something else had caught my attention. "You said *we*. Are you one of the owners?"

She nodded. "Along with my fiancé."

With Joel Stillwell? What did he know about operating a spa?

"And I promised him I'd be right back with a couple of coffees." She took a step toward the entrance. "He gets a little cranky if he doesn't get his caffeine fix."

I could relate.

"So I really do need to get going, but be sure to come to our grand opening two weeks from Saturday. And bring a friend. It's going to be fabulous!"

I was sure she believed that, but a grand opening in two weeks? Considering that Brooke and Joel were still painting, that didn't bode well for this would-be oasis to look all that grand to the well-heeled clientele they'd need to attract.

But it did help to explain why she was here, providing sustenance to her fiancé instead of her mom.

"I'll do that," I said with no intention of following through.

"Great! See you then." Brooke flashed me a smile and sashayed into the market as if everything were right in her world.

With a mother facing time in prison and a close friend recently murdered, it clearly wasn't. Yet calm oozed from Brooke's tiny pores, giving her a vibe as cool as a cucumber mask.

What was up with that?

If I was her, I would at least have developed an eye-twitch from the stress of trying to get my business off the ground.

Did she do yoga?

Meditate?

Was someone who could look that good splattered with paint even human?

My weary brain wasn't up to the challenge of solving what was going on with Brooke DeMatteo. Not without a chocolate chip cookie to go with my deli sandwich.

Okay, two.

Chapter Thirteen

"I got here as fast as I could." Based on the ear-piercing shrieks of the baby Rox was bouncing on her hip, it wasn't a moment too soon.

I peeked around the corner into her living room, where I saw the blonde who belonged to the Mini Cooper parked out front.

Since our gal pal Donna was sobbing into a throw pillow on the sofa, I was pretty sure that Rox hadn't called me to come over because she needed an emergency babysitter.

"What is going on?" And why was our favorite cosmetologist here this early on a Thursday night? I knew from all the times I had stopped by her shop that she was typically booked solid in the six-o'clock hour.

Rox motioned for me to follow her into the kitchen. "She's been like this since she showed up on my doorstep. All I know is that something happened between her and Ian."

"Uh-oh." That didn't bode well, considering that Ian was the hunky veterinarian who had slipped a diamond and ruby engagement ring on Donna's finger to accompany the dozen roses he bought her for Valentine's Day.

"Yeah." Rox grimaced as Alex buried his little head in her shoulder and wailed as if he were being neglected. "And this demon baby is being a jerk about anyone else crying in his house while he's teething. So if you'd deal with her for a few minutes while I settle him down, I'd appreciate it."

It looked to me like Rox might have the easier of the two jobs, but... "Sure."

While one miserable creature was carried to his crib at the end of the hallway, I poured a glass of water and set it in front of the other one.

"Honey," I said, sitting on the sofa cushion next to Donna. "What's the matter?"

With tears streaming down her blotchy cheeks, she waved a soggy white tissue at me as if she were surrendering. "I..."

"What?"

"I need..."

"What? Talk to me."

"I need... to blow... my nose," Donna croaked, adding the tear-soaked tissue to the others scattered around her feet.

Okay. First things first.

I handed her the travel packet of tissues I carried in my tote for interviews with bereaved family members, and then waited like I had been trained to give her some space.

But this wasn't someone else's family member I was dealing with. Ever since junior high, Donna had been one of my best friends—like Rox, the sister I never had.

So after three honks with no sign that she'd be shutting down the waterworks anytime soon, I wrapped my arm around her. "Did something happen between you and Ian?"

Donna nodded, her long, straight hair shrouding her face as she wiped her eyes.

I noticed that the sparkly engagement ring still adorned her finger, so I assumed that the wedding that was supposed to take place in six weeks was still on.

Since she had fallen head over heels in love with Ian Dearborn back when we were sophomores in high school, I sure hoped it was, or she was going to be devastated. "Did you two have a fight?"

"N-no. You have to be willing to talk to the person to have a fight."

"What do you mean? He's not talking to you?"

Donna pulled another tissue from the packet and swiped at the tear rolling down her cheek. "He's been avoiding me for days."

That didn't sound like the easy-going vet my dog loved. "I'm sure it only feels that way."

She slanted me a glare. "He cancelled on me last Friday with no explanation, then said he had something going on with Peyton all Saturday."

I'd met his daughter Peyton and knew her to be a typically active eleven-year-old. "She probably just had a birthday party or something going on at a friend's house."

Donna gave her nose another toot and then tossed

the tissue to the floor as if that's what she thought of my suggestion. "That lasted all day and all night?"

"Maybe it turned into a slumber party." Donna had to remember all the giggly sleepovers we had at my grand-parents' house.

"Then he wouldn't have been there, would he?"

Okay, she had a point.

"And then Sunday, we'd had plans to make breakfast for his mom and he cancelled that. Said Winnie was feel-ing under the weather." Donna sniffed indignantly. "But she seemed just fine when I stopped by to deliver the bouquet I bought her for Mother's Day."

Oh, dear. "You saw her?"

"Ian didn't invite me in when he answered the door, but I could hear her—them—laughing."

"Who? Winnie and Peyton?"

"Someone else was there. Another woman."

"Probably Ian's sister." I knew he had one who lived near Portland. "In town for Mother's Day. Maybe that was what was going on Saturday night—a surprise visit."

"I don't know. He just took the flowers and wouldn't explain when I asked him what was going on."

That made no sense. "He had to have said some-thing."

"Yeah, he said he'd see me Monday."

"And?"

"He came over after work, but..." Donna's sapphire eyes glistened with fresh tears. "It was weird."

"Ooh, what was?" Rox asked, bringing the clean scent of baby lotion with her as she slipped into the swivel rocker across from us.

Donna grabbed another tissue. "He didn't want to talk. He only wanted to have sex."

Rox waved her off. "Tell me about it. We're so tired at night it seems like the only time we talk is at work."

I locked on Rox's gaze to clue her in that she wasn't helping.

"Ian's not suddenly tired." Donna stiffened. "Unless he's tired of me."

I gave her shoulder a little squeeze to infuse some confidence. "There's no way he's tired of you. I've seen the way he looks at you, how he lights up when you walk into a room. So trust me when I tell you that Ian loves you."

"Then what's going on with him?" Donna cried out.

I didn't have a good answer for her. "I think that's something that you two need to talk about."

She wiped her leaky eyes. "I've tried!"

Rox gently rocked back and forth. "You need to keep trying."

"And that's been getting me nowhere." Donna turned to me. "So maybe it's time to take a different approach."

Uh-oh.

"I hate to ask," she whispered, hope gleaming behind her wet lashes.

I knew that look. I'd seen it at least a dozen times on Donna, but never once since she asked me to read her last fiancé Matt, and put him to the *test*. And never, ever accompanied by this much desperation.

Which made it a very bad idea.

I pulled away from her and focused on a carpet stain so I wouldn't have to see her disappointment in me. "I already told you how he feels about you."

"But you could find out why Ian's acting this way. Because if he's getting cold feet..." Donna gripped my hand as if she were clinging to a life raft. "Char, I need to know."

She didn't want to listen to me eight years ago, when I picked up some flirty vibes from Matt, a smooth-talker who ended up cheating on Donna with every willing female in town.

But still, I believed down to my shoelaces that she deserved to know that Rox wasn't wrong when she had thought he was coming on to her.

Ian wasn't Matt. Far from it. But...

If something really was going on with Ian that Donna should know, and I could help...

Crap. "Fine."

Donna gave me a tentative smile. "You'll do it?"

"Yes." Even though this was the same day I'd decided to avoid getting sucked into other people's drama, what was that sound I heard over Donna's squeal of delight?

Me, getting sucked in once again.

Crap. Crap. Crap.

Chapter Fourteen

Almost twenty-four hours later, Rox tossed two coasters onto the lustrous oak surface as I slid my butt onto my usual barstool. "Hey," she said over the Cyndi Lauper hit blasting through the overhead speaker. "Is Steve on his way?"

I pushed one of those coasters back to her. "Not tonight. He's working late." Probably true. Plus, I had texted him to meet me at my house so that I could have some time alone with Rox before she had to pick up Alex. "I'll order a pizza to go in a bit."

She reached for a bottle of chardonnay. "In the meantime, want the usual?"

I nodded, but what I really wanted was for her to stand still for a couple of minutes.

"Did you hear anything from Donna today?" Rox asked when she delivered my drink.

I shook my head. "You?"

"Nothing, which I hope is a good thing after how things went last night."

"I know." That was exactly what I wanted to talk to Rox about, but a couple of guys I knew from the car dealership up the highway bellied up to the bar and I had to wait until she served them.

"Okay, so what's the plan?" Rox asked when she finished working her way down the bar to me. "How are you going to approach Ian?" Then she looked over my shoulder. "Oh, hey you. Looks like you didn't have to work late after all."

Oops.

Steve kissed my cheek as he settled down next to me. "Funny how that works out sometimes."

Yeah. Funny. "I thought we were going to meet at my house."

"I saw your car out front as I drove by," he said, giving Rox a thumbs-up when she signaled him with a raised beer glass.

I needed to stop taking the first parking spot I found.

"I hadn't planned to stay very long. I only stopped by to pick up our dinner, which I was just about to order." I grabbed one of the laminated menus from the holder. "What kind of pizza do you want?"

He snatched the menu from my hand. "And thought you'd have a drink as long as you're here, right?"

I didn't like the amusement dancing on his lips. "Don't think that's a crime, Detective."

"Uh-huh. So what's the plan?"

"Well, obviously pizza for dinner and then a movie. I'll even let you pick."

"Very magnanimous of you," Steve said as Rox delivered his beer. "But that's not the plan you two were discussing."

Her eyes widened as if he had come to take me in for questioning. "I wouldn't say it was a discussion. More like girl talk, that I'm sure you wouldn't be interested in."

"Yeah, I'm sure." He reached for his glass. "Say good-bye, Roxie."

"I tried," she said on a sigh. "And on that happy note, good-bye, Roxie."

Steve took a long drink and then turned to me once Rox was busy at the register. "Want to fill me in on what's going on?"

Nope. "We were just chatting."

"About…"

I had to give him something or he was going to become even more suspicious about why I had changed our Friday night plans at the last minute.

I leaned close so that I wouldn't have to shout over the chorus of "Hotel California." "Donna. She's worried about Ian getting cold feet."

"And…"

"And needed to talk about it. You know, confide in her best friends. We girls like to do that from time to time."

"Uh-huh."

I fingered the stem of my wineglass as a distraction from the skepticism etched across the planes of his cheeks. "Anyway, she was pretty upset, but the wedding was still on as of last night." I flashed a smile to lighten the mood. "So don't think that this gets you out of buying them a wedding present."

Steve smirked. "Right. Then maybe you'd like to come shopping with me next weekend."

"Maybe I would." I should know by then if Ian was having second thoughts about marrying Donna.

"Does that give you enough time to do your lie detector thing on Ian?"

My mouth went dry. "I beg your pardon."

"That's what Rox was referring to, right?"

I looked into the depths of my wineglass for a snappy retort and came up empty. "I..."

Steve uttered a well-chosen curse word. "What are you doing getting involved in this? And when's Donna gonna grow up? This isn't high school anymore."

I didn't like his tone. "She's just confused because Ian's been giving her a lot of mixed signals."

Instead of responding, Steve took a drink.

"It's not that big a deal," I said, wishing that I could sound more convincing. "I'd like to think I'm his friend too, and if I can help—"

"Trust me. He's not going to see it that way."

That's what gave me second thoughts after I called to book a Saturday morning appointment for Fozzie.

I didn't want to insert myself into Ian's business.

Literally.

And any probing question beyond, "Are you getting excited about the wedding?" while I read his reaction would make him think Donna had sent me.

It could also lose Fozzie his favorite veterinarian, so I needed to dance very, very carefully around this powder keg.

Okay, maybe this was a big, hairy deal that I should have never agreed to. But I did. And for the sake of all our relationships, I needed to keep that powder keg from blowing up in our faces.

I wasn't the only one with a friend in this equation, so I turned to Steve. "You see Ian almost every week. He hasn't said anything to you about Donna, has he?"

"When we play racquetball after work, we play racquetball. We don't *share*."

"You are such a guy."

He shrugged. "I come by it naturally."

"Whatever. You're pretty darn good at reading people."

"Gee, thanks."

"Okay, you're almost as good as I am. When you're with him, do you get the sense that something's bothering him?"

Steve wiped all expression from his face prior to draining his glass.

I knew that he wouldn't have shifted into neutral without a reason. "I'm taking that as a yes, and Donna is right to be concerned."

"No comment."

"You didn't have to make one. I know what I saw."

He blew out a breath. "Don't read too much into what you *think* you saw."

"Why?"

"Because I don't know anything."

"Other than the fact that something's wrong."

"If there is, it's none of our business."

Actually, Donna had asked me to make it my business, but that didn't feel like a winning argument.

"Ian's gone through a lot the last two years." Losing his wife, moving back in with his mother, opening that clinic, hooking up with Donna. "It can't be easy to go through a ton of change in a short period of time. Could get to a guy."

Steve's chocolate brown eyes hardened. "You're fishing."

Yes, and he wasn't helping. "I'm just saying that he's been through a lot. So has his daughter, and maybe... I don't know." And I hesitated to take that thought to its logical conclusion. "Maybe getting married again is just too much, too soon."

"Yeah, 'again' might be the operative word here."

Okay, now it wasn't just his tone I didn't like. "What exactly is that supposed to mean?"

Steve looked over at Rox talking to a customer as if he wished she'd come back to break up this conversation. "Nothing."

"Fine. I'll tell you what I think I heard: a cheap shot at the fact that this would be Donna's third marriage."

"I'd call it more a statement of fact than a cheap shot."

"You know as well as I do that she hasn't had good luck in the husband department." Neither had I, for that matter.

"Yeah, well, maybe he's not feeling all that lucky about becoming husband number three."

"Or maybe Ian's just having pre-wedding jitters. Getting married is a big step, a lifetime commitment if we do it right."

We?

No! I should have said couples, people, anything but *we*. Because we had never talked about getting married aside from the damage control I'd had to do the last time my mother brought up the subject.

My cheeks felt like they had been torched while my racing heart lodged in my throat. "I didn't mean we...us. I meant...you know..."

Oh, dear God, make me stop talking!

Steve's lips curved with amusement, his gaze smoldering soft. "I know. And yes, it's a big step—something that you need to be very sure about."

You.

Did he specifically mean me?

Holding on to the bar railing, I tried to remember to breathe while not combusting on the spot.

"Absolutely," I muttered, nodding like a bobblehead doll. "*They* need to be sure."

And I needed to cool down before my flat-ironed hair caught on fire. I also needed to scream into a pillow. Fortunately, I had a car outside with functional a/c that could transport me home in five minutes.

Figuring that should be enough time to get my foot out of my mouth, I gulped down the last of my wine. "Okay, then. Ready to go?"

"I thought you wanted to order a pizza."

Good grief. Had my brain completely checked out? "I did."

Steve waved to get Rox's attention before she disappeared into the kitchen. Then he looked at the tables filling up behind us. "They need to get another server. There's no way this is a one-person job."

That sounded like a cue for me to offer my services. At least for those five minutes that I needed. "I'll put our order in. I assume you want the usual."

"You assume right, but I didn't mean for you—"

"I know." Sliding off the barstool, I gave him a quick smooch. "I'll be back in a few."

"How are you doing?" I asked when I found Rox emerging from the kitchen with a steaming pizza in each hand.

"Fine." She glanced over her shoulder at the wall clock glowing in blue and red neon. "I'll be doing even better when I'm outta here at six and cuddling a baby instead of pizza."

"Need any help in the meantime?"

"Char, you don't need to keep doing this. Carlos and I have this covered. Go enjoy an evening off."

For that to happen I needed to munch on a big, cheesy pizza so I didn't have to talk. "Okay if I put our order in with Carlos?"

"Like you need to ask," Rox shouted over some one-hit wonder's guitar solo as she walked away from me.

And like I needed to get anywhere near a pizza oven while I felt a bead of sweat trickling into the waistband of my chinos. Still, it gave me a break from making a fool out of myself in front of Steve.

"How's it going, Carlos?" I said, reaching for the pad

of order tickets they kept on the counter with the stacks of clean plates.

He glanced up from the sauce he was ladling onto a round of pizza dough. "Hey, I didn't know you were working again tonight."

"I'm not." I grabbed a pen to scribble down my usual order. "Rox is busy enough out there without waiting on me, so..." I tore off the ticket and added it to the queue on Carlos's worktable. "I figured the least I could do is send in my own order."

I stepped into the path of the fan blowing on him for some much-needed air. "Anything I can help you with as long as I'm here?"

He shook his head. "Not that busy yet. Thanks anyway."

I needed a few more minutes of damp-drying, so I decided to use this alone time to find out if Carlos had heard anything new about the murder. "Speaking of busy, the last time we spoke, your girlfriend was spending a lot of time over at Amity's. How's she doing?"

"Not great."

I waited for Carlos to elaborate, but he focused on the pepperoni slices he was dropping on the pizza instead.

"I can imagine." And figured that was all the news I was going to get out of him. That didn't mean I couldn't offer up some of my own. "Oh, I ran into Brooke yesterday."

He gave me the weary look I get from Patsy when she wants me to find something to do. "Oh, yeah?"

"I was surprised to see her coming out of that spa up

from the park. You know, the spa that's being remod-eled."

Carlos didn't respond with so much as a grunt as he slid that pizza into the oven.

"I didn't realize she and Joel were the new owners," I said, stepping closer so that I could gauge his reaction.

The little tug that stretched his mustache said it all. *Do I have to spell it out for you?*

I wished he would. "When did that happen?"

"Dunno. I heard Brooke talking about it at Amity's New Year's Eve party. She made it sound like they bought the place in the spring but had some setbacks getting going with the remodel."

My heart skipped a beat at the mention of Amity's name. "Setbacks can happen."

They certainly had when my ex-husband's parents remodeled their bistro. Because of the change requests my mother-in-law kept adding, a three-week project morphed into three very un-fun months.

"Yeah, Joel and Brooke tried to keep the business open for as long as possible for the income, but after the holidays they shut it down to pretty much gut the place."

After the lucrative holiday party season. Smart. They would need every penny while the spa got its makeover.

"It's comin' along now, though." He grabbed the next order ticket. "Joel brought his dad in to do all the wood-work, so it should be real nice."

Which made sense since the labor would probably be cheap. "It looked pretty nice when I drove by."

Carlos smiled for the first time since I entered the

kitchen. "Yeah, nice and fancy. Paige is already hinting that she wants to go there for her birthday. At least she'll get a family and friends discount."

"Oh, is she friends with Brooke, too?"

He nodded. "Pals through Amity. Last time we got together, the girls informed me and Trevor that we're all gonna put up flyers for the grand opening."

It was as if a shadow fell over the kitchen at the mention of Trevor's name.

"Anyway..." Carlos flattened a mound of pizza dough with a loud slap as if he were mentally kicking himself. "At least volunteering to help them with publicity gives Amity something else to think about."

"I'm sure Brooke and Joel are grateful for all the help they can get," I said to see if he'd offer up any other tidbits about the living topics of this conversation.

Given that they hadn't finished painting, getting their friends and family to pitch in was probably the only way the couple would be able to open in two weeks.

Carlos shrugged. "I guess. I'm sure they're super-grateful your mom said yes to Amity."

"*What?*"

Chapter Fifteen

I had arrived ten minutes early for Fozzie's appointment and was letting him water the weeds bordering the veterinary clinic parking lot when I got the call back from my mother I had spent the previous night waiting for.

"Hello, my darling." Marietta sounded a little groggy as if she had just woken up. "You rang?"

"Yeah, three times." Four counting this morning.

"Sorry, my phone was off. I was aligning my chakras yesterday and my agent kept calling about a script he sent me. Like he expected me to jump at the chance to get killed off in the first scene of some low-budget space cowboy movie."

It wasn't like she had been getting any better offers lately.

"Really, the man must think that I'm desperate to send me such dreck."

Maybe, but that wasn't what I wanted to talk to her about. "Mom—"

"I told him I was busy and had no desire to waste a month of my life in Romania for five minutes of screen time. Or was it Croatia?"

"I—"

"Anyway… I swear, some people are just incapable of listening."

I couldn't have agreed more. "Mom—"

"That's when you have to send them a very clear message."

That's what I was trying to do. "Yeah."

"I haven't heard from him this morning, so I think he got the hint. Although I do have several messages—"

"From me!" I said, raising my voice over the squeaky brakes of the delivery van I saw turning into the berry farm's parking lot across the street. Which was the moment I noticed Killian Havens staring at me from the entrance of the garden center.

While my mother huffed something in my ear, I pulled Fozzie close.

I'm just here with my dog. I'm not spying on you.

Much like the garden gnomes featured along the walkway near the paddlewheel, Killian stood as still as a statue. Only one that was capable of springing into action at any moment.

Despite the presence of my canine protector, this didn't feel like a good time to linger outside with only empty road separating me from a murder suspect.

"Charmaine! Are you listening to me?"

"Sorry," I said, coaxing Fozzie toward the safe harbor of the clinic. "It's loud here. I couldn't hear you."

"Where are you?"

"The vet. The one across from the berry farm." *So if anything happens to me, tell Steve where I was when you last talked to me.*

"Oh, dear. You're not calling to cancel, are you?"

"No, I wanted to talk to you about something." That would now have to wait, darn it. "You're not going anywhere until I pick you up later, are you? No hair or spa appointments?"

"No, but—"

"Good. Just keep it that way and I'll see you in a couple of hours," I said, glancing back at Killian, who was still glaring in my direction.

At least he hadn't moved, and I'd soon be in the company of people who would look a lot happier to see me.

But as he wrapped up Fozzie's examination fifteen minutes later, Ian Dearborn didn't appear to be one of them. Which was unusual, both personally and professionally, and made it challenging to chat about anything not dog-related.

"Okay, looks good," he said, shutting off the scope he had used to check Fozzie's ears. "His weight's still a little higher than I'd like to see—"

Whose wasn't? "He's like his owner. He likes his treats."

Ian looked up from his notes. "I'm sure. But I'd recommend sticking to doggy treats like dental chews, instead of leftover pizza."

Fozzie gave me a mournful glance as if he understood that last night's tidbit of crust might be his last.

Sorry, pal.

"Will do." For a while, anyway.

"Other than that, keep doing what you're doing." Ian

put away his pen and then gave Fozzie a pat on the back. "Good seeing you two."

"You, too." Recognizing that my window of opportunity to talk to this guy was rapidly closing, I locked on his gaze. "It's been a while. How've things been? Is Peyton getting excited for the wedding?"

"Sure," he said, breaking eye contact after a second of hesitation.

I didn't make much out of the hesitation because Ian knew me, and he'd be well aware that I could tell he was lying.

That's why I was surprised to hear the sarcastic edge to his voice when he added, "We're all excited."

Okay, now he wasn't even trying.

I didn't know who exactly the "we" was supposed to be in that statement, but clearly there was some problem on the Dearborn side of this future union.

And if I wanted to find out what it was, I needed to play along. "I can imagine. It's just six weeks from today, right?"

Ian's pale lips flat-lined as if we were discussing his funeral, not his wedding. "Yep."

"Donna showed me the house you found last month," I said, watching him for signs of buyer's remorse. "I love the brick exterior and the hardwood floors."

"Yeah, it's a great house. We were lucky to find it."

His delivery was flat, mechanical, reminding me of Marietta when she's running through her lines.

Why the lack of emotion? What's the problem?

Ian glanced at his watch. "You'll have to excuse me. I

have another patient waiting."

It felt more like he wanted this conversation to end, but there was nothing I could do about it beyond offering up a friendly smile.

After a wave good-bye and a brief stop at the front desk, I hustled Fozzie into my car while on the lookout for Killian Havens.

Fortunately, I didn't see anyone in the surrounding area giving me the death stare with the possible exception of my dog.

"What?" I started the ignition and lowered the passenger side window to encourage Fozzie to point that accusing snout elsewhere.

He huffed out the window and then barked as if I should offer him something tastier in exchange for the indignity of being poked and prodded.

"Hey, you're not the only one who didn't want to be here today." And I had no idea what I was going to tell Donna.

Yes, you're right. Something is going on with him, but I don't know what it is.

Some help I was.

The only insight I could offer was that there could be some trouble at home, which would only confirm to Donna that there was a reason why Ian didn't want her in the house last Sunday.

"I should have never gotten involved in all this," I told Fozzie as I pulled out of the parking lot. "Donna expects me to bring her some good news, and I've got nothing."

Fortunately, she worked Saturday mornings, just like

Ian, and she knew that I had plans to spend the afternoon with Marietta and Gram. So that gave me some time to think of a way I could put a positive spin on this.

"I'm open to suggestions if you have any brilliant ideas."

Fozzie got to his feet as we passed the red farm supply store on the corner and barked in my ear.

"Yeow, you don't have to shout."

But he wasn't listening. Instead, he jumped into the backseat to direct his doggy ire at something, or someone.

"What is it, boy?" *Please don't let it be Killian.*

After making sure my doors were locked, I glanced down the narrow lane that led to the subdivision of modest homes that had sprung up where cows used to graze back when I was a kid. But the most alarming thing I saw was the mariachi band-worthy floppy hat on the woman walking a white terrier mix.

"Seriously? You're carrying on about that puffball? You can be so... Oh!"

A girl was running to the end of a driveway to pet the puffball. "It's her." The teenager I saw on the other side of the fence last Sunday.

She'd clearly had a good relationship with Amity's dog. Which made me wonder what kind of relationship she had with Amity herself.

"Hold on," I said as I slowed to make a U-turn.

By the time I pulled up to that driveway, Fozzie had quieted with his terrier nemesis no longer in view. Unfortunately, neither was the girl. Dang it.

But I heard a lawnmower. I rolled down my window to listen. Yep, it was close by, and I only had to wait a second to see her coming toward me behind a lime green mower almost as big as she was.

She looked up and stopped in her tracks to pull her earbuds out from under her honey brown tresses. "Sorry, I didn't see you arrive," she said, scurrying over as I climbed out of the car.

I wasn't sure why she felt the need to apologize. "No problem."

As she approached I realized that the girl was younger than I had first thought. Maybe thirteen and very pretty with soulful brown eyes and cheeks the color of ripe peaches.

Before I had a chance to introduce myself, she pointed at the strip of dirt behind the *guest parking* sign. "You'll need to move your car."

She flashed a tentative smile at Fozzie when he responded to her instruction with a volley of loud barks. "Does he bite?"

"No." But I needed him to quiet down so that we could talk and reached through the open window to wrap my arm around his ruff.

"Good, because I can take him for a walk during your appointment if you like."

"I actually don't have an appointment." But her request that I move my car suddenly made a lot more sense.

Her eyes widened. "Oh. But you're here to see my mother, right?"

An adult's observations of her neighbor's behavior could be even more insightful. Plus, I doubted Mom would want to look through the lacy white curtains covering her front window to see her kid talking to a stranger. "If she's available."

"It's by appointment only on Saturday." The girl shrugged. "Sorry."

I looked past her at the sign mounted next to the arched door with the name *Harmony House* elegantly carved into the wood. "That's okay. I can make an appointment." Maybe.

But first I wanted to know what services her mother provided on the other side of that door. "Do you have a card with a phone number that I can take with me?"

"Something even better." The girl dashed to the porch and returned with a flyer in the same pale shade of lavender as the house. "This lists all our services."

"Thanks." The paper felt unusually thick between my fingers. For good reason, she'd given me two.

I tried to hand one back. "I don't need—"

"One's for your friend," she said with a knowing look beyond her years.

Okay. I figured she meant *a* friend, but whatever.

She waved good-bye to Fozzie and went back to mowing the lawn. Since her mother's next appointment could arrive any minute, I figured it was time to make myself scarce and scrambled back into my Subaru.

I reached past Fozzie to tuck the flyers she gave me into my tote. That's when I noticed *psycho* printed in a bold script font.

"Psycho? What kind of business is this?" I pulled out one of the flyers to read it more carefully.

Not psycho, psychic. Specifically, Psychic Readings. And centered below that in a smaller font: Astrology, Palmistry, Tarot, and Life Coach.

"Hmmm." I wondered how Detective Pearson felt about interviewing a psychic. He had to have talked to her along with most of the neighbors.

I would have loved to have been a fly on the wall for that interview. Knowing how much Steve hated hearing Marietta talk about anything the least bit "woo-woo," I could almost imagine Madam Harmony House playing with a deck of tarot cards just to mess with Pearson's head.

Still, real or not, someone advertising herself as a psychic had to be pretty intuitive. Observant, too, which could be a handy quality in the murder investigation of her next door neighbor.

Maybe an appointment with the woman was exactly what I needed—preferably an appointment that I could tag along on so that it wouldn't look like I was trying to get answers from the great beyond.

And I knew just the person who could benefit from some life coaching: Donna.

I could promote a visit to Harmony House as a much better alternative to me trying to grill Ian for information, especially since that plan had already failed.

Yep, I could swing by with a flyer...

"One's for your friend."

"Whoa." A prickle of awareness crawled up my spine

as I watched the kid disappear into her backyard with the lawnmower. "How'd you know?"

Chapter Sixteen

"Seriously," I said, staring in disbelief at the people rushing toward my car. "You called ahead?"

I hadn't needed to ask. It was obvious by the welcome sign that Neil and Dorothy Constantine were holding.

"Just to make sure that someone would be available to help me with my purchase." Marietta crawled out of the backseat and waved at the small crowd gathering behind that sign. "How kind you are to make such a fuss for little ol' me."

A fuss that she had clearly prepared for, since her hair and makeup were picture-perfect.

The family members and customers waving back at her consisted of some of the same faces that I had taken pictures of last Sunday, so maybe my mother had done me a favor by arranging this photo shoot.

We'd have to hang around the farm supply store for at least an hour, and I had every intention of making the most of it.

Fortunately, one of the Constantine family members I had wanted to chat with seemed content to play hostess to Gram and me—*after* she had her picture taken with my mother.

"Your mom's a real sport to pose for pictures with everyone," Leah Constantine Latimer said, leading Gram and me through the deserted store to her office.

My grandmother turned to me. "One would almost think it was planned."

Was she suggesting that Marietta's insistence that we get here by twelve-thirty to have plenty of time for lunch was in any way a setup? "Yep."

Turning on her office light, Leah stepped back from the doorway. "I hope you don't mind that my mom is monopolizing your mother's time. She's a big fan."

Was she kidding? That fandom combined with my grandmother's aching feet provided us the perfect excuse for us to sit and talk without interruption.

"I appreciate you letting us wait in your office," I said to Leah when she wheeled in a chair for Gram from the next room.

"Just don't look at the mess." Leah grimaced at the stacks of paper strewn across the surface of her metal desk. "Despite what my dad might think of my system, there's a method to my madness when it comes to paying the bills."

"No worries." I didn't care what Neil thought unless he had an opinion about who murdered his nephew.

She took a swipe at her overly long bangs as she settled into her desk chair. "Are you sure you don't want to sit?"

"I'm fine." I was leaning against the wall, around three feet away from her, which afforded me the perfect location to both observe her and keep an eye on the door in case her brother Spencer wandered back. Because I was dying to ask Leah how he got that black eye.

"Can I get you some coffee?" She pushed back from her desk. "I got here a few minutes before you did, so I can't guarantee how fresh it is."

I could smell it cooking from where I was standing and shook my head to signal to Gram that we didn't need to guzzle any bitter brew. I also didn't want Leah to feel compelled to offer us anything but some conversation.

"I'm sure we've had enough caffeine for one day," Gram said. "But thank you anyway."

"Plus, we're planning on going to the tea room next door for lunch a little later. My mom missed out on Mother's Day." I figured the reference to the day of the murder might elicit a reaction.

Leah nodded, dropping the polite smile that had been hanging from her lips the last few minutes.

And there it was.

"Just as well," I added. "I'm sure her presence would have only added to the curiosity seekers that day."

She sighed. "I'm sure."

"It was bad enough that I had to hang around all afternoon. It felt so intrusive." Which was true, but no more intrusive than what I was doing here in her office.

"Yeah, I saw you talking to the police." Leah rested her elbows on her desk as she looked up at me. "I have to admit, though, that I wasn't sure it was you, not until I noticed you talking to Eleanor."

Since Leah had gained at least sixty pounds since

high school and now wore square, thick-framed glasses, I wouldn't have recognized her either.

"It's been a long time." I angled to get a better view of the family picture on the corner of her desk. "I see you have a little boy now. Cute kid."

She brightened. "And spoiled rotten, especially by his grandmother."

"That's a grandmother's prerogative," Gram said, giving me a wink.

"I'm sure Leah's mom would agree with you and probably loves every minute she can spend with *all* her grandchildren."

"Actually, it's just Ethan." Leah turned the picture so that Gram could see the cutie holding his mom's hand.

"Oh, for some reason I thought Spencer had kids." Only because it helped me get back to the subject of his shiner.

She scoffed. "Hardly."

"He's young," Gram chimed in. "There's plenty of time to start a family."

"Time might not help him." Leah lowered her voice. "Don't get me wrong. I love my little brother, and he does great with the things around here that don't talk back. But with women he's like an undomesticated beast."

I aimed a glance at the doorway to ensure we were alone. "Don't tell me that's how he got that black eye."

"Uh…" Leah blinked. "He ran into something."

Sure.

"I heard it was Trevor's fist," Gram offered up as if it were hot dish from Duke's Cafe.

Courtesy of her sister, no doubt.

Leah stared at the pile of bills in front of her. "It was nothing. Really."

Considering that Trevor ended up dead, I didn't need to look at her to know she was lying.

Still, I channeled my best Marietta imitation by touching my fingers to the base of my throat to feign surprise. "Oh, my gosh! They had a fight?" *Do tell.*

Her heavy brows furrowed. "More like a discussion that got a little out of hand."

A little.

"And I don't think we need to say any more on that subject," Dorothy announced from the doorway prior to giving me a wary glance. "Your mother is test-driving a riding lawnmower. She wants you to join her out back and shoot some video of it."

Dang. My mother's timing was almost as bad as her driving.

"Oh, dear." Gram got to her feet. "I hope Neil is helping her because she shouldn't drive."

"She's behind the buildings in open field," Dorothy said. "She's fine."

"That's what you think. She's not nicknamed 'Mayhem Moreau' for nothing!" Gram rushed out the door with Dorothy falling in step behind her.

Standing, Leah looked relieved to focus on someone else's family member. "Is she serious? Your mom drove that DeLorean all the time on her old show."

On a closed set and under ten miles an hour. "Don't spread it around, but most of the time it was a stunt driver."

"Your secret is safe with me." Leah stepped toward the door. "I won't even tell my mom. Wouldn't want to ruin it for her."

"Speaking of your mom, I'm sorry if I brought up a sore subject." And since this was probably going to be my only chance to talk with Leah one-on-one, I had to bring it up again. "I know this a really difficult time for your family with Trevor's decision to put the business up for sale. I assume that's what prompted that *discussion*."

Her jaw tensed, disgust tugging at her lips. "Well, that's not a very well-kept secret."

I didn't want to be the one to tell her that her mother made the mistake of divulging it to Alice. "You know how the rumor mill works around here."

Leah shook her head. "Doesn't matter. I'm sure the smug look on Amity's face tells everyone all they need to know about what's going on."

"You make it sound like Amity's the one who convinced Trevor to sell."

"Oh, I know for a fact that she is."

Clearly, Leah was on the same page as her mother. "And she inherits..."

"Everything."

"All the property, the equipment—"

"She's made it very clear that he left her everything."

I inched closer. "You don't think that she had anything to do with his murder."

Leah expelled a stale breath as she headed out the door. "I don't know what to think, but I made sure that

Detective Pearson knew that Amity isn't the innocent widow she's pretending to be."

That sounded like a yes to me.

Chapter Seventeen

"I declare, Mama," my mother huffed in her annoying just-off-the-plantation accent while we watched Neil park the lawnmower back in the storage barn. "You can be the biggest killjoy. I just wanted something fun to show Barry."

"You call what you were doing in that field fun?" Gram lowered her voice. "You practically mowed down Neil."

Which is why I had kept my distance. I didn't want to give my dumb dream a chance to become a premonition.

"That wasn't my fault." Marietta pointed at me. "Chahmaine should've warned me that he was standing there. After all, she was right next to me with the camera."

Excuse me? "You were driving! That means that you're supposed to look where you're going."

Gram wedged between my mother and me like a referee at a wrestling match. "Enough. Fortunately, there was no harm done."

"And everything worked out just fine." Jutting out her chin, Marietta slanted me a glance. "Despite what some people may think."

"So, Miss Marietta," Neil announced, striding toward us in the same kind of work boots I saw Killian wearing last week. "Are you ready to sign on the dotted line?"

She brightened as if Mr. Constantine had shone a spotlight on her for a closeup. "I am indeed. I'm sure mah husband will just love that cute green one."

The crow's feet at the corners of his eyes crinkled with pleasure. I couldn't tell if it was because the woman with the ridiculous accent had just pointed out his most expensive lawnmower or if it was that she thought it was "cute."

"I'm sure he will." Mr. Constantine gestured toward the main building. "Shall we?"

Marietta clapped her hands together with glee when we exited the store ten minutes later. "Delivery has been scheduled for the afternoon of Barry's birthday, then Charmaine will come over with the cake." She beamed at her mother. "I love it when a plan comes together!"

Gram tried to shoo her toward the parking lot. "That's nice, dear. Let's go eat."

My mother stuffing food in her face instead of rattling on about this birthday sounded good to me.

But instead of pointing her studded platform sandals toward my car, she stepped in the direction of the red Corvette parked in front of the house at the end of the drive. "Nice car. Whose is it?"

"No one you know." And I intended to keep it that way.

Marietta narrowed her eyes like Gram's devious tabby

cat seconds before he'd swat me with his tail. "You say that like you don't want me to know."

Because it had taken almost the entire drive over here to convince her that I should handle the arrangements for her opening-day appearance at Le Calme.

"No, it's just that it's no one that we need to disturb." *And no one that you need to involve yourself with.*

Gram hooked her arm. "Char's right. Let's go."

Digging her sandals into the loose gravel path, Marietta sucked in a breath. "That house is where that murder took place, isn't it?"

There was no denying it. "And the person who lives there is grieving, so—"

"Let's all give her some privacy," Gram said, finishing my sentence for me.

"Her?" Marietta shielded her eyes from the overhead sun, improving her view of the woman stepping down from her porch. "That one with the pink hair? I know her."

Seriously?! Couldn't Amity have stayed in her house for another two minutes?

Setting off in her direction, Marietta waved. "Well, hello there."

Amity stopped, meeting my mother halfway down the drive. "Hi, this is a surprise."

"Indeed. How fortuitous to bump into you again." Marietta motioned for Gram and me to join her. "Allow me to introduce my mother, Eleanor, and my daughter, Chahmaine."

Wearing a tangerine tie-dyed T-shirt over the same

frayed jeans, Amity looked like a peace-loving hippie as she shook Gram's hand. But there was nothing peaceful about the hard stare she aimed at me. "Hello again. I had no idea that Marietta was your mother when I met her the other day."

"Good to see you again." And there was no need for either one of us to say any more than that because this needed to be a short conversation.

"I didn't realize that the two of you already knew one another." My mother turned to me. "Now I see why you wanted—"

"To follow up about what you'd need from us for my mom's upcoming appearance," I interjected before she made me sound like a stalker. It was bad enough that I was standing outside of Amity's house. Again. "Not that we need to discuss publicity matters now. Because I'm sure you're busy and we were just about to—"

"I'll call you." Amity eased back in her flip-flops as if she were just as eager for this impromptu meeting to break up as I was.

Then someone moving at other side of the fence caught my eye and I understood why she didn't want us here.

Because that someone in the backward baseball cap wasn't going to pretend to believe that I wasn't stalking them. Not when he'd seen me twice in the last three hours.

Unfortunately, after we said our good-byes, our next destination was his mother's tea house, where I spotted Killian glaring at me from the kitchen doorway.

Lovely. That made it three for three.

I didn't know if he had anything to do with the murder, but if looks could kill I'd be the next one to go.

"Okay." Marietta nudged my shoulder. "That boy has been skulking about in the shadows for the last hour. Who is he?"

Again, no one I wanted to discuss with her, especially since Killian's mother could reappear with our lunch order at any minute. "The owner's son. And he's hardly skulking. He works here."

"Well, he's quite attractive and seems to be paying particular attention to you. Does Steve have reason to be jealous?"

"Why?" Gram glanced back over her shoulder. "What's he doing?"

I cringed, slumping in my seat. "Nothing." And mercifully, Killian was no longer in view. "Let's talk about something else please."

Marietta smiled at her mother over the rim of her teacup. "I think my daughter doth protest too much about her admirer."

The only thing I wanted to protest was the mouth she wouldn't shut. "Mom—"

"Allow me, honey," Gram said. "Mary Jo, you don't know what you're talking about because that boy is certainly no admirer of Char's."

My mother's cup landed on its saucer with a clatter. "What do you know that I don't?"

Gram leaned in to whisper. "He's the one that Char saw creeping around that house the last time we were here."

Marietta turned to me. "He's the one?! But I thought that person was arrested."

I shushed her. "He was *questioned*. Just like we were all questioned."

"Oh, don't make it sound like it's the same thing. I did plenty of investigatin' on my show," she said as if those three years made her an expert. "There's questionin' of witnesses and then there's questionin' of suspects."

"Well, it's not my investigation, so all I know is that a bunch of us were questioned."

My mother reached for her teacup. "No arrests have been made yet?"

"Nope." At least none that I had heard about through the gossip circuit.

"Really. That seems incredibly slow." Marietta paused to take a sip. "We didn't have the benefit of DNA evidence and mainly just used our feminine wiles back in the day, but by the end of each episode we always had our man."

In her case, usually in more ways than one. "This isn't TV. Real-life investigations take time."

She scoffed. "You're sounding more and more like Steve."

Gram smiled at me. "Take it as a compliment, honey."

I was pretty sure it wasn't intended that way. "All I'm trying to say is that, to the best of my knowledge, the investigation is still ongoing."

"I highly doubt that's the extent of your knowledge," Marietta remarked, slanting me a glance.

Excuse me? "What's that supposed to mean?"

She looked down her pretty nose at me. "I saw the way Amity was looking at you."

Like she wanted me to leave before her ex-husband arrived to pay her a visit? "She was just surprised that we were related."

"Oh, my darling." Marietta gave her head a little shake. "It was more than that. She was annoyed to see you back at the scene of the crime, given who you work for. That cool 'I'll call you' of hers was a dead giveaway."

It was more of a brush-off, but I wasn't going to nit-pick. At least we weren't talking about Killian any longer, which was perfect timing because his mother was step-ping out of the kitchen with our sandwich order.

"It reminds me of that episode where the bad guy's lady accomplice recognized me while I was sharing a sauna with her. That look of hers told me that my cover was blown. Of course, with one of the girls rifling through the guy's desk, I had to chase her down in my towel to keep her from tipping him off."

Of course.

"I loved that episode," Gaylene chirped, placing chicken salad croissants in front of Gram and Marietta. "I always wondered. How'd you keep that towel on while you were running?" She winked at me while handing me my turkey club. "I can't keep one from slipping off when I'm standing still."

"Safety pins along with a tie thingee sewn into the towel." Marietta flashed a demure smile. "I was wearing a one-piece underneath, so the towel was actually much less risqué than it looked. You know, decorum."

Said the woman whose wet T-shirt poster was a top seller that year. "Right."

"You always wore the most *interesting* costumes," Gaylene responded in my mother's defense.

Most of the boys at school didn't use that adjective when referring to my mother's lack of attire, but I could see that Gaylene was as big a fan as Dorothy next door and stuffed my face with my club sandwich so that I didn't ruin the moment.

Gaylene stepped back, clutching her empty serving tray to her white apron. "And I don't mind saying, you're the best thing that's happened to us all week."

Marietta tittered. "Oh, you're too kind."

"No really, look at this place." Gaylene swept her gaze across all the empty tables behind us. "It's a ghost town. It has been ever since..."

Frowning, Gram dropped her sandwich to her plate. "It's been like this all week?"

"Ever since poor Trevor was killed," Gaylene said, her eyes pooling while her voice hitched with emotion. "And Killian..."

"Oh, honey." Gram slid onto the next chair and motioned for Gaylene to join us. "This has to be so hard on you and Rory."

While Gaylene settled in the seat across from her, Marietta mouthed to me. "Who's Killian?"

This was no time to bring her up to speed. "Tell you later," I whispered.

"It will get better once they catch the guy," Gram said,

handing our host a napkin to dry her eyes. "You'll see. Everything will get back to normal."

"Normal." Killian's mother wiped the tears spilling over her sparse lashes. "I hardly remember what that feels like."

Gram gave me a nod as if to suggest that it was my turn to offer the woman some encouragement.

What was I supposed to say? Her son looked guiltier to me every time I saw him. "These things take time."

Marietta gave me the same disparaging glance I got when I didn't cheer the idea of her marrying Barry and moving a thousand miles closer. "But they always sort themselves out. Take my show, for example."

Oh, let's not. "Absolutely. Things will sort themselves out...eventually." Whether the Havens family could find some sort of normalcy when that happened was another matter entirely.

Because if Killian had returned home to Port Merritt to exact some sort of revenge...

Gaylene buried her head in her hands. "If only he hadn't come back for that dog."

The dog?!

Chapter Eighteen

My grandmother dropped her handbag on the kitchen table and then headed straight for the wine rack next to her toaster. "What a day. I know your mother wanted us to stay for dinner, but her perfume was giving me such a headache I couldn't take anymore."

I pulled the lapel of my peach slouch shirt to my nose. "I can still smell her. I'm gonna have to take a shower when I get home." Or Fozzie would shun me since he hated Marietta's musky jasmine as much as I did.

"You don't need to rush off right away, do you?" Gram held up two wineglasses. "Because I've been dying to ask you about something."

"I bet I know what it is," I said, pulling the corkscrew from her top utensil drawer. Because she had barely said a word since we left the tea room. "The dog."

"Because Gaylene made it sound like Killian didn't want any trouble. You heard her. He only wanted his dog back."

Yep, I'd heard her, but I also saw how hard Gaylene was working to convince us. Like she needed to believe it herself.

She had also left out something. "Maybe. But I doubt that the shouting match between Killian and Trevor was over the dog."

Leaning against the counter, Gram gave me a hard stare as I uncorked the wine. "You think it was about Amity."

"Don't you?"

She grabbed the bottle as if her patience were wearing thin and started pouring. "That seems to be the consensus today."

What? "Who are you referring to?"

"Dorothy."

All right, Gram!

I carried our glasses to the kitchen table, where I wanted my grandmother to make herself comfortable and tell me everything she knew. "I was with you all day. When did this happen?" Because I had wanted a few minutes alone with Dorothy Constantine but could never pry her away from shadowing Marietta.

"When you were chasing your mother around that field with your phone." Gram took a sip of Chablis and then smiled contentedly. "See, it pays to get old so that you're forced to watch such foolishness from the sidelines."

"Yeah, I can hardly wait. So, what did she have to say?"

"She caught a glimpse of Amity looking out her window at us, and I guess that set Dorothy off. She just launched into a tirade about that girl biding her time until she ruined them."

"By selling the business." This was old news and she knew it. "I already heard that through Alice."

Gram's face flushed as she fingered the stem of her wineglass. "Oh … uh … Alice may have mentioned something about Dorothy confiding in her about that. But what she doesn't know…"

I felt like injecting a *yet* but took a drink instead.

"Is that Dorothy heard her nephew warn Killian to stay away from his wife."

I wondered if this was the same argument that Gaylene had witnessed. "When?"

"Dorothy didn't say, but she made it darn clear that she thought they were in cahoots together."

Something was going on between Killian and Amity. That was for sure. They had a bond. I had picked up on it the instant that he stepped into her house.

Did that mean that I thought Killian was the one who drove that knife into Trevor's heart? He sure didn't act the least bit guilty when I caught him stepping down from that porch last Sunday. He just looked like a guy who was happy to see that his dog was okay.

"What do you think?" Gram asked.

Whatever answer I gave her would become tomorrow's hot topic at Gossip Central, so it was best to admit to nothing. "I don't know."

She scowled at me at the same time that her doorbell rang.

Saved by the proverbial bell. "I'll get it."

"We're not done here," Gram called after me. "I want answers."

So did I. Fortunately, the guy who might be able to provide some was smiling up at me from her porch. "Hey, I saw your car outside."

"Good, 'cause you're just the man I wanted to see," I said, pulling Steve close for a quick peck on the lips.

Screwing up his nose, he shut the door behind him. "And not the woman I wanted to smell."

I groaned. "I know. I'm taking a shower as soon as I get home."

"If you need someone to scrub your back, I'm in." He fingered the neckline of my shirt. "Then, if you insist, you can have your way with me."

"Well, aren't you easy."

"Not that easy. You'll have to feed me too."

"I'm sure that could be arranged if you answer something for me."

Steve pulled back, his eyes shuttered. "Here we go."

"Don't take that tone. You haven't even heard what I want to ask."

"I don't need to, Chow Mein. I know where this is going."

"Okay, smart guy, what was I going to ask you?"

"Gee, I don't know. Since you took your mother to that berry farm today, it's probably about something that happened in the vicinity."

"How did you know that? I only told you that we were going shopping."

"And your grandmother mentioned where when I mowed her lawn this morning," Steve said, setting off for the kitchen.

I followed him. "Then she has a big mouth."

"I heard that," Gram declared. "And it's not like we have any state secrets around here."

Which was exactly why I didn't tell her anything that I wasn't prepared to share with Steve. "Well, we don't have to broadcast our every move."

Steve settled into the chair across from my grand-mother. "One might think she's trying to keep something from me."

I was.

"Not at all," Gram said. "In fact, we're glad you're here because we were just talking about Trevor Constantine's murder."

Steve glowered at me. "Were you now."

I grabbed one of the beers that she kept in her refrig-erator for him and set it on the table. "Be nice."

"I'm always nice." Steve twisted off the bottle cap. "Doesn't mean that I can add anything to your discus-sion, though."

"Sure you can." Gram pointed an arthritic finger at him. "Because I need you to explain why Killian Havens hasn't been arrested."

"Well, Eleanor, I would assume that it's because there isn't enough evidence to charge him."

She shook her head as if that wasn't a satisfactory answer. "There were words exchanged between him and Trevor. Threatening words."

Steve shrugged and took a swig of beer.

"Dorothy Constantine told me they practically came to blows."

Gram was laying it on a little thick. I could tell from the little smirk playing at the corner of Steve's mouth that he thought so too.

"'Practically' isn't something that typically gets you arrested," he gently pointed out.

"I know, but..." Gram turned to me for help. "You saw how Gaylene acted today, like she needed to defend what her son had done."

"Yep." It didn't mean that he was guilty of murder. "Anyone who spends any time there can see that something's going on with him."

Steve stared at his beer. "Maybe."

"Maybe?!" Gram slapped the table with the palm of her hand. "Darn it, Stevie! Everybody knows that Killian Havens is involved in what happened last weekend. Wouldn't surprise me a bit if his ex put him up to it. It could even be a murder for hire kind of thing."

Steve slanted a glance in my direction. "Interesting discussion I walked in on."

"We heard some interesting things today," I told him.

"I bet." He sharpened his gaze. "I'm sure none of it was at all solicited."

"I beg your pardon. Are you suggesting that my grandmother and I took my mother out shopping for the sole purpose of soliciting information?"

Steve reached for his beer. "I would never accuse your granny of such a thing."

I stuck my tongue out at him.

Gram frowned at Steve. "I wish you would take this more seriously."

"Not my case, Eleanor. But I'm sure the detective in charge is taking it very seriously."

"But has he talked to Dorothy Constantine?" Gram asked. "Because she told me herself that she thinks that Amity and her ex are in cahoots."

"*Cahoots*?" Steve took a long swig from his bottle. "Kind of hard to prove cahoots in a court of law without proof."

She aimed that frown at me. "I don't like his tone."

Welcome to my world.

"I know. Put the attitude aside for a minute, and let's say for the sake of argument that there isn't any proof that Killian Havens and his ex-wife planned Trevor's murder. Don't you find it suspicious that Killian moved back in with his parents, who happen to live next door to Trevor and Amity. I mean, come on. That's gotta raise an eyebrow. And then a week later..." I looked at Gram because I wasn't sure that timing was right. "Two weeks later?"

"I thought it was two but couldn't swear to it," she said.

"That should be easy for someone to find out." I leaned in to get a good read of Steve's face. "Anyway, within days of Killian showing up next door to where his ex-wife is living with his dog—that according to his mother he wants back—Trevor Constantine is murdered. You don't seriously think that's a coincidence, do you?"

Steve locked onto my gaze as if this were a reprise of one of the staring contests from our childhoods. "I don't know."

He was telling the truth, but that didn't mean I had to like it. "That's not a good-enough answer."

"Sorry, Chow Mein. That's all I've got for you." He drained the bottle and then pushed away from the table. "Thanks for the beer, Eleanor. If you'll excuse me, I've got some things to do before I lose daylight."

Steve headed for the front door without giving me a second glance.

Wait a minute! I thought he was coming home with me. "But you're still coming over for dinner," I said, catching up with him. "And other stuff, right?"

"I don't know." He lowered his voice. "I guess that depends on what you have in mind."

"You know exactly what I have in mind because you put it there."

"So I did. Are you done with your interrogation?"

For all the good it did me. "Yes."

Steve pressed his lips to mine. "Good. Because you reek and probably need to get out of those clothes right away."

My pulse did a happy dance at the thought of him peeling them off of me. "That sounds like that might lead to something."

"Not here it doesn't, and I don't see you moving," he teased, stepping onto the porch.

I ran back to kiss Gram on the cheek. "Gotta go!"

Chapter Nineteen

I had just returned home from attending church with my grandmother when my phone rang.

"What do you wanna bet that's Steve?" I asked the furball greeting me at the door.

Since Steve could have looked out his front window to see me drop Gram off, I hoped he was calling with an invitation to Sunday brunch.

Then I promptly lost my appetite when Donna's name lit up as the caller ID.

I pointed the phone at my dog. "Want to take this?"

Fozzie gave it a sniff of disinterest, then padded over to claim the sunshine warming the hardwood next to the sliding glass door.

"At least one of us knows when to stay out of Donna's business."

Dropping into my loveseat, I pressed the phone to my ear. "Hey, I was going to call you later." Much later.

"I couldn't wait," Donna said over a rumble of road noise.

"Where are you?"

"At Hot Shots."

That espresso stand was located a block from the waterfront—clear across town from her apartment—which made me think that she didn't pick Hot Shots for their coffee.

"Want to join me?" she added. "Or do you have plans?"

"No plans." Plus, I was going to have to talk to her sometime.

Wanting to get it over with, the second I disconnected, I grabbed a jacket to ward off the wind from Merritt Bay, and drove down to the waterfront.

After parking near the Feathered Nest gift shop, it didn't take me long to spot Donna waving at me from one of the two picnic tables behind the espresso stand. At least I thought it was her, because with the pulled-up hoodie hiding her blond hair and her oversized sunglasses, she looked more like an escapee from a witness-protection safe house.

"What is this?" I asked, giving Donna a hug. "Are you going incognito this morning?"

"No." She glanced back at a passing car before reclaiming her spot on the bench seat. "I just don't want it getting back to Ian that I met with you."

I took the seat across from her so that I wouldn't have to look into the sun. "We're friends. We see one another all the time, so I don't think that's something you need to worry about."

"Easy for you to say. Unless there's something that you learned yesterday that helps explain what's been going on with him."

I shook my head. "Sorry. I tried."

Donna swore under her breath. "Now what do I do?"

I knew what I had wanted her to do, but now that I was sitting in front of her, suggesting that she seek a psychic's advice felt incredibly self-serving.

"Let me get myself a latte and let's talk about that." Because I needed a couple minutes of think time before I offered her any advice.

She picked up the tall to-go cup by her side and placed it in front of me. "Here. I got you a mocha latte."

So much for that think time. "Thanks."

"No problem. It's the least I can do for dragging you down here. Because really, Char, if I didn't have you to talk to—" Her voice broke as she reached into a pocket for a tissue. "I don't know what I'd do."

But I wasn't the one who could provide her with what she needed. "I wish I could help. I really do. But honey, Ian's the one you need to talk to—"

"I've tried! Over and over again."

"What about counseling?"

Donna lifted her sunglasses to wipe her eyes. "He refused to discuss it, and told me to stop worrying. As if everything's fine. Trust me, everything is *not* fine!"

That was certainly the impression Ian gave me yesterday. And if he wouldn't talk to someone about it, maybe she should.

I wasn't so sure that person should be a psychic, but it felt like the time had come for me to lay my cards on the table.

"Okay, this may seem completely out of left field," I

said, placing a Harmony House flyer in front of her. "But I went by this place yesterday after Fozzie's appointment with Ian."

Donna took off her sunglasses to read it. "You went to a psychic?"

"I only stopped by for a second. And that's part of the reason I'm bringing this up. Now hear me out before you say anything."

"A psychic who does counseling. Why didn't I think of this?"

Donna was getting way ahead of me. "I can't vouch for—"

"Oh, don't worry about that. Rox and I went to a psychic in Seattle a million years ago. Her predictions weren't all super-accurate, but the stuff she ended up being right on was incredible."

"What? Where was I when this happened?"

Donna shrugged. "I don't know. Away at culinary school, I guess. Anyway, she told me that I shouldn't marry the first guy who asks. Boy, was she right about that."

I pointed at the image of the house on the flyer. "I don't know that this one can offer anything the least bit helpful to either one of us, but I want to go sometime soon and ask her about something."

"Ooh, wanna go together?"

I smiled at the sunlight dancing in Donna's sapphire eyes. "Only if you're sure this is something you want to do."

"Are you kidding?" She grabbed her cell phone. "Let's

find out when she has an opening," she said, punching in the number. "What do you want? A reading?"

All I wanted was some time. "Whatever is cheapest."

After an exchange of greetings, it became apparent to me that Donna had some preliminary questions to ask the woman, so I walked to the pier with my coffee to give her some privacy.

Not five minutes passed before I could hear the gulls gathered on the pilings squawking their protests at the arrival of another human with nothing in her hands to feed them.

"We're in luck," Donna announced. "She can see us today."

"When?"

"In an hour."

I almost choked on my latte. "An hour!"

"You said you didn't have any plans, right?"

"I know, but..." It suddenly felt like we were rushing into something, and for Donna's sake I didn't want it to translate into a decision she'd later regret.

"You want to do this with me, don't you?"

"Definitely."

"Yay! I think this could be really enlightening."

I sure hoped she was right.

Chapter Twenty

"I love what they've done with this place," Donna said, taking off her sunglasses as I pulled in front of Harmony House's guest parking sign. "The last time I drove by here it was for sale, but it sure didn't look like this because this is downright charming!"

"Yeah." It looked a lot like the lavender and lace version of the house from one of Marietta's more recent horror flicks. All charm on the outside to lure in unsuspecting visitors, but in the basement where the bodies were buried, it was an entirely different story.

Donna couldn't stop smiling as we climbed the steps to the front porch. "This is gonna be great."

I wished I could share her optimism. "If nothing else, it will be interesting."

Just don't go into the basement.

Before I could knock, the girl who had provided me with the flyers swung open the white-painted door.

Her warm brown eyes swept over Donna, her lips curving with satisfaction when she shifted her gaze to me. "Hi. Did you bring your dog?"

"No, he's at home," I said.

Her smile slipped a little. "If you come again, remember that I can walk him."

Since I had a dog walker around her age, I wondered if this kid had offered the same service to Trevor or Amity. "I brought my friend, though."

She gave her a little wave. "I'm Donna. I'm the one who called."

"I'm Clio." The girl stepped back and made a sweeping gesture as if she had been well-trained. "Please come in. My mom's expecting you."

We entered a tiny foyer covered by an oriental area rug in rose, ivory and blue, complementing the creamy raspberry mousse on the walls. A bouquet of fresh lavender graced a dark cherry console table under a wall clock chiming the hour.

"It's this way," Clio said, leading us down a carpeted hallway lined with white framed pastels of wildflowers and pastoral landscapes. Not at all the beads and baubles decor I had been expecting.

Something was cooking in the sunny kitchen we walked by. Something beefy with plenty of cumin and garlic that overpowered the scent of the vanilla votive candle flickering on an antique washstand at the end of the hallway.

Again, nothing here struck me as new agey or particularly unusual. Harmony House looked and smelled more like a homey bed and breakfast than a home to anyone in the business of summoning spirit guides.

Clio gestured toward the large room to the left of the washstand, where a petite woman in her fifties rose from behind an uncluttered desk. No computer, no photos, no paper. Just an oversized deck of cards occupied the surface.

"Welcome," she said with a friendly smile. "I'm Harmony Peel."

Dressed in yoga pants and a blue broad-striped caftan that almost came to her knees, Harmony had warm golden brown eyes, much like her daughter, cheeks with a healthy glow, and streaks of silver in the soft curls that framed her round face.

Extending her hand, she stepped toward Donna in butterfly print slipper socks. "Donna, I assume." She didn't wait for confirmation that she had guessed correctly. "It's good to meet you. Would you like to go first?"

Donna smiled nervously at me. "Why not."

Harmony turned to her daughter. "Cliodhna, please show Charmaine to the waiting room. And give the chili a stir."

"We don't really have a waiting room," Clio whispered to me after she clicked the door shut. "It's just the living room, but you can watch TV there if you want."

What I wanted was to hang out with her for most of the next hour. "I don't—"

"Want some tea?"

I opened my mouth to reply, but like her mother, Clio didn't wait for an answer and led me into a tidy kitchen with a white and gray star-patterned floor, and a stove that was probably older than I was.

She pointed at the pedestal table in the corner. "You

can sit over there and I'll bring it to you." She opened a white cupboard door to the left of where the pot of chili was simmering next to a steaming kettle. "We have green tea, lemon balm, peppermint, and some nasty saffron herbal stuff."

She reminded me of me at that age. I hated everything with saffron too.

"Green tea is fine." Plus, it was probably the only thing in that cupboard with caffeine.

While Clio filled a ceramic mug from the kettle, I looked around the kitchen for something that I could use as a conversation starter. "The chili sure smells good. Who's the cook, your mom?"

Gliding toward me in scuffed sneakers, she kept her gaze locked on the very full mug in her hands. "Yep."

In the hallway, I had noticed a family picture with a jowly guy sporting a military buzz cut and two kids, a gap-toothed Clio and an older boy. "Nice place. Is it just the two of you here?"

"Right now. My brother's at Western."

A lot of the local college-bound kids went to Western Washington University. It was close enough to drive home for every holiday and a lot cheaper than the UW in Seattle. Still, I wondered what kind of money this psychic made to be able to afford the tuition.

"He got a scholarship," Clio added with the same knowing look as yesterday.

She didn't offer any other information, so I assumed that the military man belonged to the folded flag encased in glass above the washboard.

"How long have you lived here?" I asked when she picked up a wooden spoon to stir the chili.

"Since August."

"It seems like a nice neighborhood. My grandmother and I come out here a lot. She especially likes the tea room at the berry farm."

Clio glanced at me as if she were waiting for me to get to the point.

"You might have seen us next door. We were here Sunday."

She stopped stirring. "I know."

What else do you know?

"I had to hang around that afternoon because of what I saw earlier."

Her eyes widened. "What?"

I didn't want to mention Killian in case she had become friendly with him. "It was more what I heard — their dog was barking like something was wrong."

She fidgeted with the spoon as she stared into the pot of chili. I was making her uncomfortable.

Sorry, kid. I know it's tough to talk about.

I picked up my mug of tea and carried it over to the white laminate counter to better see her face. "It was really loud. I bet you could have heard it from here."

"We weren't home."

"So you didn't see or hear anything unusual that day?"

"We got home after," she said, her chin trembling while tears filled her eyes. "You know, *it* happened."

Probably true, but that didn't answer my question.

It also didn't matter because I'd just made a child cry. It was time to talk about something else.

I leaned back and sipped my tea to give us both a breather. "Their dog sure seemed happy to see you. I think it helped calm him down when you came to the fence."

She wiped away her tears with the back of her hand. "Max is a good boy. He hates being in that cage, though."

"So would my dog."

"That's because they need to be able to run around."

"And go for long walks. Fozzie loves his walks."

"So does Max, but he goes a little crazy when he sees another dog."

That sounded like she was speaking from personal experience. "Do you take him on walks sometimes?"

"Uh..." Her lips disappeared. "Sometimes."

What about walking her neighbor's dog did she not want me to know?

"That's nice. I have a friend who walks my dog too. She used to do it every day when I lived in an apartment near her," I said, staring at a glass bowl filled with oranges and a kiwi while I racked my brain for a way to get this teen to open up. "Now it's just sometimes, when the weather's nice. I never know how much I should pay her. How much do you charge?"

Clio blinked as if I had asked her a trick question. "I don't do it to get paid. Max and I are friends."

"This last week has to be hard on him too. You know, because dogs can sense when something's wrong."

Dropping the spoon in the pot, she jerked back as if

I'd pulled a knife on her. "Why do you keep talking about that? Are you a cop? Is that why you were there that day?"

"No. I told you. I was there because I heard Max and thought he was in some sort of trouble."

"And now you're here because you think I had something to do with it," she cried, running out the back door.

"No! It's not like that."

Shoot! If I wanted Clio Peel to confide in me, I was going about this all wrong.

I followed her past a raised bed of leafy green veggies, into the corner of the yard, and then gingerly approached where she was sitting on a tree stump with her knees clutched to her chest. "I'm sorry. I can do a little of what I think you can do. I read people, and I can sense their emotions."

Although her face was shrouded by a veil of honey brown, she didn't shrink away from me so I inched a little closer. "Sometimes that leads me to ask too many questions. My grandmother calls it sticking my nose where it doesn't belong." So did Steve, for that matter. "But if I can help figure out what happened next door, it feels like the right thing to do."

After mopping up her tears with the hem of her cotton candy pink T-shirt, Clio peered up at me. "I try to help people too. My mom says it's our calling."

I assumed that meant Clio was a psychic in training, and hoped I could call on her to help me.

Wishing there was room for me on that stump so that we could confide in one another girl-to-girl, I did the next best thing and hunched down as far as the snug waistband of the olive green slacks I'd worn to church would allow. "So, you can see what brought me here today. I'm just trying to help."

She shrugged a thin shoulder. "I guess."

That was far from a ringing endorsement. But after pumping her for information the way I did, I didn't blame the kid for her lack of enthusiasm.

"A big way you could help is to tell me if you noticed anything different—anything or anybody that seemed *off* that morning."

She wrapped her arms around her knees again like she needed something to hold onto. "Not really."

That would be a yes.

"Maybe Max was barking a lot, or maybe you were back here," I said, pointing toward where I had seen her standing by the fence. "And you saw or heard somebody."

"I saw Max, but..." Clio buried her face in her knees. "It's not a big deal."

From the guarded way she was acting it looked like she thought it might be a very big deal. "Would you tell me? Maybe it could help us figure this out."

"It might get me into trouble." She snuck a peek at me. "So if I tell, you have to promise not to talk to my mom about it."

"I promise." But if her mother was a psychic with any real ability, she probably already knew all of this kid's secrets.

"Okay," Clio whispered conspiratorially. "I went over

there that morning to visit Max. I do that sometimes when I know that Amity isn't around."

I had a feeling that this might be a long story and wished I had worn something more comfortable as I dropped to my knees. "Where was she?"

"I dunno. She left a few minutes after I came out to water." Clio pointed at the raised bed that bordered the tiny patio. "That's when I heard Max barking about getting put in his cage, so I hid behind the big tree by the fence to see what was going on."

It seemed that there was a lot of lurking behind trees that day.

"Then she drove away," Clio said.

"By herself?"

She nodded.

So far I hadn't heard anything that should get her into trouble. "Then what happened?"

"Max was barking and barking 'cause he hates being left alone in that cage, so I climbed over the fence to keep him company. I know I'm not supposed to. Amity got mad the last time I did that and I ended up getting grounded."

"Then Amity probably isn't the one who lets you walk Max."

Clio hung her head. "She doesn't like me hanging around."

That couldn't have been just because she'd caught the kid trespassing. "Why do you say that?"

"That's pretty much what she told my mom. Like I'm some sort of snoop. Just because I saw... Never mind."

No! She couldn't stop there. "You saw something that Amity didn't like, huh?"

Clio nodded.

"I've seen some things over there that Amity didn't like, too."

Clio stared at me like an unblinking owl. "You've seen her with *him*?"

"You mean Killian, the guy that works at the berry farm?"

She nodded.

I did the same.

"What'd you see?" she asked.

"I saw them hug one another, kind of like married people do."

"I saw them kissing before Amity drove off," she said, her voice mainly breath.

Holy smokes! "Kiss, like on the lips?"

Clio looked at me like Steve does when I suggest watching a chick movie. "Yes, on the lips."

Okay, I told myself, leaning back on my heels. That didn't mean that Killian and Amity plotted Trevor's murder. It only looked that way a little more every day.

"Did you tell the sheriff's detective this when he talked to you and your mom?"

She shook her head. "I didn't want to get anyone into any trouble."

By the worry etched across her delicate brow, I knew that she meant the trouble that she'd be in with her mother. "That's okay. There's plenty of other people around here who think Killian might be involved in what happened."

"But he's not," she stated with a certainty that made my skin prickle with gooseflesh.

"How do you know that?"

"I just know."

Then this psychic in training had quite a lot more confidence in Killian's innocence than I did.

"What about Amity? Do you think she might have had something to do with it?"

Clio shrugged. "I dunno."

"Me neither. The only one back there that I know is absolutely innocent is Max."

She glanced over her shoulder. "I miss him. I haven't given him a hug for a whole week."

"I'm sure he misses you, too," I said, remembering her petting him through the fence. *Wait!* "You gave Max a hug? Sunday morning?"

"I always give him hugs when I see him."

Which would require opening the door of that doggy play pen.

Maybe that was the main reason that Amity had complained about the kid. Clio hadn't exhibited suffi- cient respect for boundaries. "I didn't realize that you let him out of his cage."

"I didn't. Trevor came out of the house. All fast like. I thought he was gonna yell at me. I think he thought I was somebody else."

Since Killian had been there minutes before, I didn't have to guess who.

"When he saw it was me, everything was cool." Clio's

pretty brown eyes misted again. "He told me Amity wouldn't be back for a while and gave me the leash to take Max for a walk."

"What time was that?"

"I dunno. Around eleven, I guess."

"Then what?"

"Max and me walked around the block. We would've gone longer, but my mom was taking me shoe shopping, so I had to get back."

"Okay." That meant that she would have returned with Max sometime around eleven-twenty. I shivered with the realization that she could have been there the same time as the murderer. "Was anyone at the house besides Trevor when you and Max got back?"

She shook her head.

"Did it seem like anything was wrong?"

I got another head shake. "He was just making breakfast."

"You *saw* him making breakfast?"

"Well, he called it breakfast. It just looked like he was cutting up some weird fruit to me."

"Fruit?" I asked, my heart pounding as I recalled what Shondra had said about seeing food on a cutting board.

"Yeah, after I put Max back in his cage, he gave me a slice. It was really good."

Holy cannoli! This was probably mere minutes before Trevor was killed. "Then what happened?"

"Nothin'. I said bye to Max and went home."

"You didn't see anyone else around?"

"Nuh-uh."

"And that's it. Nothing else happened?"

She thought about it a second. "Trevor gave me some of the fruit to take home. I didn't think I should take it at first. You know, in case Amity thought I stole it or somethin'. But he said he had a lot and was gonna be getting more."

"Still, that was nice of him."

"He was nice." Clio started tearing up again. "Really nice."

"Out of curiosity, was the fruit a kiwi?"

"It was!" She sucked in a breath. "You must be psychic too."

Hardly. I'd seen a bowl of kiwis when I was in that kitchen, so it wasn't much of a stretch to identify the "weird fruit." It just didn't help me get any closer to solving the mystery of who killed Trevor Constantine.

Chapter Twenty-One

"It's your turn," Donna announced when she joined me in the living room twenty minutes later.

Dropping my notebook in my tote, I pushed out of the chintz chair facing the front window, where I had been scribbling down every detail that Clio told me about last Sunday.

"How'd it go?" One glance told me that I didn't need to ask. Donna's face radiated with joy.

"It was incredible."

"Incredible as in useful or entertaining?"

"Both. You just wait. You're gonna be amazed."

"Uh-huh." I didn't need amazement, just some honest conversation.

"Charmaine?" Standing in the hallway, Harmony Peel called out my name like a nurse at a doctor's office. "I'm ready for you now."

I wasn't so sure that I was ready for her, but I painted a polite smile on my face and followed Harmony back to her office.

Faint notes of vanilla from the votive candle drifted in the air even after she shut the door, providing the only scent that I could detect coming from her direction. Since there were no candles in Harmony's office, no fresh-cut flowers, no potpourri, and she wore no perfume, I assumed that she preferred to conduct business with a minimum of olfactory distraction.

"Please." She waved a graceful hand at one of the two burgundy wingback chairs across from her desk and then took a seat.

Unlike the other rooms in the house, an accent wall the color of grape jelly was behind her. The three other walls were in a soft ivory the same shade as the window coverings, and were adorned by framed family photos and kid's artwork. Under a foot-long rainbow that I suspected Clio had painted a few years back, a Boston fern on a bamboo plant stand occupied the corner behind me.

The only light illuminating the room filtered in through the Roman shades, which created a restful mood, but wouldn't help me see her micro-expressions, so I scooted the chair a little closer. "Hope you don't mind."

"Not at all." Harmony folded her hands on her desk and met my gaze. "Make yourself comfortable."

I forced myself to release the iron grip I had on the arm rest. Probably as comfortable as I was going to get.

"Now then," she said with that same knowing look that I had seen in her daughter. "How may I help you, Charmaine? Or do you prefer Char?"

Was she asking because she had heard Donna refer to me that way? "Char's fine."

Leaning back, Harmony squinted at me like Donna does when I'm overdue for a haircut. "How have you been sleeping, Char?"

The bags under my eyes shouldn't have been any worse today than any other day. "I sleep as well as most everyone."

"Not lately, you don't." She extended her arm as if she could wipe away some invisible film above my head. "Your aura is a muddy yellow. You take a lot upon yourself. I see quite a bit of stress. Maybe think about cutting back on the caffeine."

Her level of specificity based solely on first impression wasn't bad. At the same time, given how common a factor stress was in life, it was a low-risk observation to make. And Donna could have mentioned calling her from an espresso stand, clueing her into my caffeine addiction, so I had yet to share my pal's amazement in her abilities.

"Okay." The next time I was offered tea, it wouldn't kill me to go for the herbal stuff.

Harmony folded her hands again as if resetting herself to neutral. "So, what brings you here today?"

"I have something that I wanted to discuss with you."

She smiled, waiting.

"I was in the neighborhood last weekend when your neighbor was killed."

Harmony nodded, registering no surprise at my mention of the murder. "Ah, you're the one."

"The one what?"

"The one with the name beginning with C. You have a

strong connection to some people here. I've been feeling your presence all week."

Did she really expect me to believe that? I had just volunteered the information she had parroted back to me.

"I don't know that I'd call it a strong connection. But I've seen and heard some things this week that make me wonder if Amity Constantine could have been involved in the murder of her husband."

Harmony stared straight ahead with unfocused eyes. "Yes, I can see why you might think that. But no, she didn't kill her husband."

"How about hiring someone to kill him?"

"No. That's not the vibe I get."

"Is that how this works? You get a vibe?"

She gave me a nod. "That's the easiest way to describe it. But it's kind of like watching snippets of a movie. I get flashes of images."

"Okay, then what vibe do you get about who killed him?"

"Mainly that he's someone he knew. That struck me almost right away."

"So you see a male?"

"Not a face, but it's male energy that I'm picking up along with a lot of anger."

"You know Killian? He's been working the last couple of weeks at the berry farm. Forty-ish, dark hair." Full of pissed-off male energy.

"Not personally, but I know who he is."

"What do you think of him?"

She did the unfocused stare thing again. "There's a darkness in him. Long simmering anger that feels on the verge of erupting. And... Oh." Her gaze sharpened. "You've seen it too, and very recently."

Harmony turning her third eye on me caused my heart to skip a beat.

"Not to worry," she added with a flick of her wrist. "He's not mad at you."

Could have fooled me. "Who's he mad at?"

"The world? It feels like a long list."

"Was Trevor on the list?"

"Without a doubt."

That sounded more like a declaration than a vibe. "You sound very sure."

"I have ears and could hear those two shouting at one another just fine. I'm quite sure."

"Okay. Since tensions had been building, let's say that Killian went to the house Sunday to have it out with Trevor. We know he was seen there around the time of the murder."

Harmony's dark eyelashes fluttered for a split second. "By you. Ahh, that's the connection."

"I just happened to be there because I heard—"

"The dog. Yes. He was drawn there for the same reason. Because he sensed something was wrong."

She could have gone to the Havens farm for one of the tomato plants I saw on her patio and heard about the dog from Gaylene. And she could have seen me talking to Detective Pearson and put two and two together.

Nothing in her body language gave her away. Not so

much as a glimmer of satisfaction lit her eyes as she watched her words wash over me. Instead, Harmony cocked her head as if she had just received news from some invisible messenger. "You saw that in him, too."

Oh, she was good. Extremely skilled at masking her emotions while reflecting back to me the tidbits of information she had picked up over the last several days.

Or there was a much more complicated reason for everything Harmony had told me: She had abilities beyond my comprehension and believed every word she said.

That didn't mean that I had to.

"I'm more interested in what you actually observed around here," I said. "Did you see or hear anything that made you think that Killian could have something to do with the murder?"

"No, nothing. Like I said, that's not why he was there."

That made two residents of Harmony House who seemed convinced of Killian Havens's innocence.

"Okay, if he didn't do it, what else can you tell me about the murder?"

Leaning back, Harmony closed her eyes, the stripes covering her ample chest scarcely rising as she breathed. "It's time," she finally said. "I hear him saying that it's time."

"Time for what?"

"I'm not sure. I just keep getting something about time."

Me, too. That I was wasting mine to think that she

could tell me anything useful.

"Perhaps we can get some clarity from the cards." She picked up the deck of tarot cards in front of her and handed them to me. "Please shuffle as many times as you'd like and then place the deck back on the desk."

I felt as though Harmony was inviting me to go down a rabbit hole with her. "I don't know that I believe—"

"It helps me focus." She smiled, her voice buttery soft. "If you wouldn't mind."

Fine.

I shuffled the deck three times and returned the deck as she had instructed.

Without hesitation, Harmony arranged cards in front of me one after another. "Okay," she said, pointing at a card called the Hanged Man. "He was caught in a situation of his making." She moved her hand to the next card. "He made choices but those choices had dire consequences."

"He who, the killer?"

She nodded. "He thought he was on the right course, but the Moon in reverse tells me that he was deluding himself. Given what we know about what happened, that makes sense."

If Harmony expected me to agree with her, he wasn't the only one indulging in delusion.

"The Queen of Swords in the future position suggests that another decision point is coming."

That sounded like a very safe prediction to make. "What's that supposed to mean *exactly*?"

"I think you'll recognize it when you see it."

"Me? I thought we were talking about the 'It's time' guy."

"Like I said earlier, you have a connection," Harmony said in a firm tone, as if she were telling me this for my own good. "I'm pretty sure that's why you're sitting there today."

"I'm just trying to get some answers."

"Some are easier to come by than others, but perhaps I can do one more thing to help in that regard." She pointed at my left ear. "Do you wear those earrings fairly often?"

I didn't like where this was going. "Yes, why?"

"Indulge me," she said, extending an open palm.

I unhooked one of the twisted gold hoops Steve bought me last June for my birthday and dropped it into her hand.

Making a fist as if she were at a Vegas craps table, Harmony lit up like I probably did when I opened his present. "Oh, he loves you."

I didn't know how to respond. This wasn't what I was here for.

She tilted her head as if she were listening to that messenger again. "A name with an S?"

Holy crap!

No. Before my pulse leapt into the stratosphere and I bought all this mumbo-jumbo, I had to keep in mind that Donna likely mentioned Steve during her hour in this seat.

"A protector but also a friend. Yes, he's the one. I see a wedding in your future."

That was a gimme since Donna came here to talk about her wedding.

"Wrongs of the past have shaken your confidence. Trust was broken. You've been letting this hold you back." Harmony gave me a nod of encouragement. "It's time to let it go."

Let go.

Move on.

Don't let your past define your future.

Yeah, yeah, yeah. I could get the same level of pithy advice from my daily horoscope.

"I see you with a cup in your hand," she said.

So did I, every dang day.

Harmony handed me my earring. "That's when answers will come."

In other words, she had nothing for me.

But coming here hadn't been a total loss. Using Clio's input I would be able to create a pretty accurate timeline for the day of the murder. And Donna was the happiest I'd seen her all week. That alone was worth what the last twenty minutes were going to cost me.

"I know you're disappointed, but before we can reap, we must allow our garden to grow. That's where you are right now, but your intuition is strong. You'll be ready when it's time."

I wasn't just disappointed, I was getting annoyed with all her cryptic references to time. "Okay."

Harmony pulled out a cell phone with a credit card reader from a top drawer. "That's all we have time for unless you'd like to book another twenty minutes for a more personal reading."

"No, thanks." I'd had quite enough.

A couple of minutes later, after we exchanged good-byes with Clio and Harmony, Donna linked her arm with mine as we stepped off the front porch.

"What'd you think?" she asked, pulling me close. "The stuff she came up with was amazing, right?"

"It was interesting."

"That's it? Just interesting? Didn't she seem to know stuff without you telling her?"

"Yeah, but some of it probably came from your conversation with her."

Donna jerked back. "What do you mean by that?"

"Just that you could have mentioned Steve so—"

"Why would I mention him? I came here to talk about the guy I'm supposed to be getting married to."

"So you didn't give her any information about me?"

Donna smirked. "Honey, I didn't pay her a hundred bucks to talk about you."

Then the last twenty minutes might have been a little more interesting than I had thought.

Chapter Twenty-Two

After tossing and turning most of the night, I trudged into my kitchen around three with Fozzie, grabbed my notebook, and started to work on that timeline.

By the time I'd sucked down half a pot of coffee and the darkness beyond my kitchen window turned to a predawn smoky gray, I had developed a fairly clear picture of everything that happened in the hour prior to Trevor Constantine's murder. I even knew what he had been eating, but what good did that knowledge do me?

It didn't get me any closer to knowing the identity of the person who came to the house after Clio left.

And given all the weird stuff I had seen and heard over the last week, that bugged the heck out of me.

Throwing down my pen, I could almost hear Harmony's voice echoing in my head.

It's time to let it go.

"Sure," I said, waking up the dog that had been snoring at my feet. "I could do that."

Just as I planned on cutting back on the caffeine like she had suggested.

Since that clearly wasn't going to happen today, I

dragged myself into the shower, and got ready for work. Then, after coaxing Fozzie into the backyard with a biscuit, I headed over to Duke's to distract myself with a couple of hours of baking (and eating).

"Uh-oh. This can't be good," my great-aunt Alice lamented when the kitchen door banged shut behind me a few minutes before six.

Duke looked up from the oatmeal he was measuring into a stainless stock pot. "Shouldn't you be in a nice warm bed right about now?"

"Top of the morning to you too," I said on my way to the coffee station.

He grunted. "You know, if you drank less of that stuff you'd probably sleep better."

"So I've heard." And didn't particularly want to hear it again this morning, especially from the guy who liked to brag that his inky brew could double as jet fuel.

Returning with the carafe, I refilled their cups, all the while aware that Alice had been watching my every move from her worktable. "I suppose you have something you'd like to add."

"Would it do any good?"

"Nope."

Resignation tugged at the corner of her mouth as she reached around a muffin pan for her cup. "I knew you were gonna say that."

"I guess I'm not a woman of mystery then," I said, grabbing a mixing bowl from the shelf behind her.

"Not if you're here to bake because you can't sleep."

"Maybe I just had a craving for your chocolate chip

cookies."

"You know good and well that you're early for cookies. Gotta get this last batch of muffins in the oven first."

"Then you're lucky I'm here to save you the time."

"Yeah, lucky." She grimaced at me over the rim of her cup. "It's that murder, isn't it. That's why you can't sleep."

"I just have a lot on my mind."

"You know you can talk to me if something's bothering you."

And tell her that I couldn't stop thinking about what a psychic predicted was in my future? She'd blab to Duke about it before my coffee cooled. Then he'd be sure to tease me about it in front of Steve at his earliest opportunity. "I'm fine."

"You don't seem so fine to me," she called after me as I pulled on one of the white aprons that had been hanging on a hook near the door—the same door that Lucille was entering.

"Look who's here." She aimed a predatory smile at me. "Just the person I wanted to talk to."

"Good luck with that," Alice said. "She's not in a talkative mood."

"Then she came to the wrong place." Lucille squeaked by me on her way to her locker. "Because she and I need to have a little chat."

"What about?" *Please don't let it be about me.*

"Well, I was shopping yesterday and ran into Estelle," Lucille said, lowering her voice to a stage whisper as she stripped off her mango orange cardigan. "She bumped into Margie Doyle at the library, or was it the drug store? You know Estelle, she's a talker. It's hard to keep up when she gets goin'."

It took one to know one. "And?"

"Anyway, Estelle heard it from Margie, who heard it from Sylvia, who was talking to Dorothy after church yesterday that Neil and Spencer aren't speaking."

"Really." Maybe that accounted for the fact that I didn't see Spencer within fifty feet of his father on Saturday. "Did she say why exactly?"

The puckers around Lucille's persimmon-painted lips deepened. "Why do you think? Spencer blames his dad for the big stinkin' mess they're in. Says none of this should've happened. That Neil should've made Trevor sell him the business."

"I heard that had been in negotiation." Since my informant was sitting less than twenty feet away, I lowered my voice. "I didn't think his dad had that kind of money, though."

"He doesn't."

"Then what did Spencer expect?"

"I dunno. For his dad to be some sort of miracle worker? And when that didn't happen, I think the kid took matters into his own hands. And we all know what happened after that."

"Yeah, I heard about the fight he and Trevor had after a family meeting."

"Oh, I'm pretty sure that fight didn't end that night." Lucille slammed her locker as if that should be the last word on the subject.

"Wait a minute." I grabbed the carafe and followed her out the swinging kitchen door to the coffee station. "You think that Spencer Constantine murdered his cousin?"

"I'm certainly not rulin' it out," she said, grabbing a white porcelain mug from a rack under the counter. "Think about it. He had a beef with the dude, *and* he had motive and opportunity. Could've been in and out of there in two minutes."

True enough, but... "If his fingerprints were on that knife they would've arrested him by now."

She arched her sandy brown eyebrows. "You'd have to be pretty dumb to not wipe down the knife. Spencer may be a hot head, but he ain't no dummy."

And Dorothy had been very quick to cut off our conversation about Spencer yesterday.

"What about his mom?" I asked, filling Lucille's cup. "Do you get the sense that she thinks he's *that* much of a hot head?"

"Dorothy's protected that boy all his life. Made excuses for him every time he got kicked out of school for fighting. Let him live at home for-flippin'-ever. Heck, she had to bail him out after he got arrested for mixing it up with Steve way back when."

What? How is it I never heard about that?

"She tried to make it sound that it was just boys being boys." Lucille shook her head. "But in her heart, I think she knows. Spencer is just one of those guys that trouble seems to find."

That was certainly the feeling I got that day he sold me

the chicken poop. "Criminy." I had been looking at Amity and her ex-husband so hard that I hadn't considered Spencer Constantine to be a serious suspect until now.

"You can say that again." Lucille took a slurp of coffee. "If I were a betting woman I'd wager that another arrest is in Spencer's future."

Since he fit Harmony's description of the murderer, I wouldn't bet against her.

"Looking for something in particular?" Stanley, one of the cafe's more senior regulars, asked after I sat next to him at the counter an hour and a half later and picked up the Sunday regional newspaper he had been scouring.

Stanley was a wiry, white-haired, retired Boeing engineer, who devoured newspapers the way that Fozzie scarfed down every tidbit that landed in his dog bowl.

But Stanley also liked to stick his big nose into everyone's business, and I didn't want him sticking it into mine. Not when I knew that Steve could be dropping in for breakfast any minute.

"Just looking," I said.

Stanley leaned close as I rifled through the pages to find the obituary section. "For someone you know?"

"I'm just checking on something." Specifically, the date and time of Trevor Constantine's funeral service, but his name was nowhere to be seen.

"What are you two lookin' at?" Lucille asked, topping Stanley's cup off with fresh decaf.

I folded the paper and picked up my spoon to eat the

oatmeal I'd barely touched. "Nothing."

He reached for the sugar. "She was checking out the obituaries. No one I knew was there. Can't say the same for her."

"I bet I know who she was lookin' for. But hon, they're not gonna have anything in the paper that we don't already know about him," Lucille announced loud enough for almost everyone in the diner to hear.

Stanley froze with the sugar shaker poised above his cup. "Who are you talking about?"

She leaned in, the points of her platinum bob curling into her cheeks. "Trevor Constantine, who else?"

"Shhh!" I didn't need this discussion getting back to Steve, Frankie, Shondra, or anyone else I worked with.

"Am I interrupting a meeting?" Steve asked, sliding onto the stool next to me.

Crap!

Dropping my spoon in my bowl, I forced a smile. "Don't be silly. We were just talking, and we're done now." Very done.

Lucille scowled at me and then set an empty cup in front of Steve. "You want the usual?"

"Sure." He turned to me while she reached for the carafe to fill his cup. "Or do I need to order extra bacon because I'm gonna have to share some?"

I heaved a sigh. "I don't want any of your bacon." In the last hour I'd already consumed two cookies, three strips of bacon, and a bite of the buttery scone I'd packed in my tote for a mid-morning snack. I didn't need any more grease in my system.

"Uh-huh. Then you must have had your fill before I got here."

Loving a guy who knew me as well as he did had its drawbacks. "Whatever."

"So," Steve said, dumping creamer into his coffee the instant Lucille squeaked to the window to deliver his order. "What was it you were saying about Trevor Constantine?"

"It was just about his obituary not being in the paper." Stanley winked at me through his horn-rimmed glasses. "Charmaine here suggested that the family might not want the additional publicity, given the nature of how he died and all."

Thank you, Stanley, for taking one for the team.

"A reasonable conclusion, no matter who made it." Steve took a sip of coffee and then frowned at something on the front of my favorite cotton knit tunic.

"What?" I asked, trying to see what he was looking at.

He brushed it away with his napkin. "Cookie crumbs?"

There was no denying the evidence. "I came in early and helped stock the bakery."

"Uh-huh. Looks like something with some chocolate chips didn't make it that far."

"Don't be the food police. It was breakfast."

He pointed at my bowl. "Then what's this?"

"Second breakfast."

"No wonder you don't want any of my bacon. So what got you up so early?"

"It was just one of those nights."

"If you'd cut back on the caffeine you'd probably sleep better."

Good grief. "That seems to be the rumor that's going around."

"Oh, speaking of rumors," Lucille said to Steve while splashing coffee into our mugs. "Someone brought up the subject of that dustup you had with Spencer Constantine a few years back."

He gave me a side-long glance. "Someone?"

I shook my head. "I'm innocent."

"I know better," he whispered in my ear.

"Wait. What dustup?" Stanley asked.

Steve reached for another creamer cup. "It was nothing."

Lucille scoffed. "If memory serves, you had to arrest the dude, so I wouldn't call that nothin'."

"Oh, yeah," Stanley said between slurps of decaf. "I'd forgotten about that."

Steve stirred his coffee. "Why are we bringing up ancient history?"

"Order up!" Duke bellowed.

Lucille returned the carafe to the warmer behind her. "Because we all know that it's relevant to the investigation into Trevor's murder."

Steve turned to me the second Lucille left to pick up her order. "'We'?"

"You have to admit that Spencer Constantine has a reputation for some anger management issues."

"I don't have to admit anything." Steve reached for his coffee.

"And it's not your case." I waved him off. "Yeah, yeah, we know. I would imagine that Detective Pearson would have to be well aware of Spencer's history."

"Chow Mein." Steve made my nickname sound like an admonition.

I injected enough sugar into my smile to put him into a diabetic coma. "Yes?"

"We're done talking about this."

I dropped the smile. "You may be, but I'm not."

Blowing out a breath, he swiveled around and headed for the door. "Come on."

Once my feet hit the sidewalk, I had to run to catch up since Steve had already made his way to the corner. "Where the heck are you going?"

"Here." He unlocked the gunmetal gray Ford pickup parked next to my Subaru. "Get in."

"Sheesh," I said after I climbed into the bucket seat. "Is the cloak and dagger approach really necessary?"

"You tell me." He folded his arms across his chest. "You're the one who wanted to talk."

"Only because I was at the farm supply store a few days back and Spencer was acting kind of suspiciously."

"What were you doing there?"

"If you must know, I was picking up something for my grandmother."

Steve gave me a long look. "Right."

"Anyway, he had a black eye and I happened to ask him about it, and he got all defensive."

"Probably because he didn't want to talk about something that was none of your business."

"He didn't want to talk about it because Trevor was the one he had the fight with."

Steve's expression didn't change.

I wasn't telling him anything he didn't already know, just like the other night. "Okay, I get that he wouldn't want to talk about it, but don't you find the timing kind of suspect?"

"That you went back over there to see what you could find out? Yeah."

"You're being intentionally evasive."

"And you're involving yourself in something that you need to stay out of."

"But Spencer had motive and opportunity." I couldn't believe I was actually quoting Lucille. "He's a hot head who could have snapped when he found out that Trevor was selling the business."

"Are you through? 'Cause I have a breakfast I'd like to eat before it gets cold."

"I wish you would take this more seriously."

"Chow Mein, I seem to have to remind you that this isn't my case to solve. It's not yours either."

"But—"

"Let it go," he said, punctuating his words with a quick kiss.

It was the same advice Harmony Peel had given me. Just a lot harder to hear.

Chapter Twenty-Three

Three hours later, I had just caught up with the filing when I noticed that I had received a text from Donna.

Can you meet Rox and me for lunch?
I have big news!

Since Donna had seemed so happy when we left Harmony House, I hoped for her sake that her big news translated into good news about Ian.

I texted her back to suggest an eleven-thirty lunch at Eddie's since I had a one o'clock deposition to get back to. Until then, I had several background checks to run for Shondra's upcoming case. And as long as I had the database open, I entered the name of the person I most wanted information on: Spencer Constantine.

Within seconds I had the date of the assault and disorderly conduct charge that earned him a brief stay in the county jail. Since Steve had been the arresting officer and the incident happened outside one of the more popular bars in town, it wasn't a surprise that Lucille and Stanley had known about the "dustup." But the lack of other criminal history was.

If trouble liked to find Spencer Constantine, he didn't have any other arrests to show for it.

After running an internet search that made it look like Spencer lived off the grid, I ran a search for Killian Havens.

From what I could piece together, Killian had been living in Alaska most of the last ten years, where he'd worked on an oil rig as an electrician. Married Amity Riggle from Juneau six years ago. Divorced five years later. No children.

I found zippo criminal history for him in the database, and like Spencer, no social media.

So everything that I read about these two guys made them look more like loners than murderers in the making. But they had both been acting like they had something to hide since the moment Trevor's body was discovered. Why?

I could find no answers online, and I had already reached out to a psychic who made it sound like I needed to have a cup in my hand for all to be revealed.

Fine.

I picked up my coffee cup, closed my eyes, and offered the question up to the universe: *Who killed Trevor Constantine?*

"If you need something to do, file these," Patsy said, dropping a short stack of manila files in my inbox.

That was so not the revelation I was looking for.

✳

"Please tell me that Donna and Ian are gonna be okay," Rox said, slipping into the seat across from me now that Eddie had taken over at the bar.

I closed my browser after searching in vain for news of Trevor's funeral service and set aside my phone. "She told me yesterday that she knew what she needed to do." Beyond that, Donna hadn't wanted to talk in the car, which was fine with me since my head had been spinning ever since we left Harmony House.

"You look annoyed. What is it you're not telling me?"

A lot.

I didn't want to spill about consulting a psychic since that should be Donna's story to tell. So I opted for the one thing Rox might be able to help me with while we waited for Donna's arrival. "It's nothing. It's just that I can't find any information about Trevor Constantine's funeral. Since I know the family a little, I thought I should go."

"I don't think you're gonna find any announcements about that. From what Leah was telling me Saturday, Amity hasn't wanted to do any of that kind of stuff, which is really ticking off the rest of the family. I guess they finally talked her into holding a private service at Tolliver's. She mentioned that Constantine Farm Supply was closing early for it, so it must be late this afternoon."

"Dang." So much for that idea.

Rox grinned. "You just wanted to go in case someone decided to make a public confession?"

"I don't think that's likely to happen." But she wasn't far off.

"I bet Lucille was hoping that it would. That woman loves herself some good funeral drama. Plus, she's just as much of a snoop as you are."

"I beg your pardon."

"It's true and you know it."

This was not a moment I needed the truth thrown in my face. "There she is," I said, grateful to turn my focus to Donna as she made her way to our corner table, her long hair cascading over the ruffles of her floral print blouse.

"Sorry I'm late." She smiled at me. "Did you tell Roxie anything about where we went yesterday?"

"I was waiting for you." And had no desire to give Rox more ammunition about the lengths I had been willing to go for information.

"Okay, good." Donna gave Rox a squeeze and then dropped into the chair between us. "You'll never guess what we did yesterday. We went to a psychic!"

"You've got to be kidding me," Eddie chortled as he set three tumblers of water on the table.

Rox glared at her husband. "No one was talking to you or will be talking to you later if you say another word." She turned to me. "Do you know what you want?"

After Donna and I ordered a couple of salads, Rox shooed Eddie away. "Okay, as you were saying before we were so rudely interrupted. Where'd you go? Seattle?"

Donna shook her head. "She's just outside of town, at Harmony House, over by Ian's clinic."

"I didn't know there was one over there."

"It's that cute lavender-colored house," Donna said

between sips of water. "Down that side road."

Rox's eyes widened. "The one behind where Trevor Constantine was killed?"

"Well, yes." Donna shook her head. "But that had absolutely nothing to do with why we went there."

"Sure it didn't," Rox said, leveling her gaze at me.

"She does counseling, and since Char wasn't able to get any information out of Ian Saturday, I thought that Harmony could provide some fresh perspective. And did I ever get some! We both did, although one of us doesn't want to admit it."

"Yeah, I got to hear all about my muddy aura. So Donna may have gotten more out of this than I did." Certainly more than what I cared to discuss. "But it was definitely interesting."

Donna sighed. "Interesting doesn't begin to do it justice. It was fascinating. Harmony knew stuff about me—specific stuff. And I didn't even have to tell her about Ian. She said she could sense I was troubled."

Probably because Donna started crying as soon as she sat down in that wingback chair.

"So what'd she have to say?" Rox asked.

"That I wasn't imagining that there was a problem. But she said that it's a problem that Ian hasn't known how to solve because it's coming from outside influences." Donna glanced over her shoulder at a couple taking one of the other tables, and dropped her volume to a whisper. "Specifically, his former mother-in-law."

I stared at Donna in disbelief. "She's making trouble about the wedding?"

"The only thing Ian said when I asked him if he'd heard from her lately was that she was at the house on Mother's Day. So hers was the other voice I heard that day."

So? "I get if she's not crazy about the idea of him re-marrying, but what makes you think that Harmony's right about why he's been acting funny?"

"Because ever since Melody got to town, Ian's been different. He hasn't wanted to talk, hasn't wanted to do anything but jump into—"

"We already know that part," Rox interjected, clearly no more eager to hear about their sex life than I was.

"Anyway, it's obvious that she's responsible for what's going on because... Here, I wrote down what she said during my reading." Donna pulled a slip of paper from her pocket. *"A harbinger of darkness recently arrived and she needs help to overcome her fear of it."*

"Ooh." Rox looked at me. "That's what I'm gonna start calling my mother-in-law—a harbinger of darkness."

"Be serious," Donna protested. "This has become a real problem."

It sounded too ridiculous to be taken seriously. "Why the heck would Melody be afraid if she's the one bring-ing the darkness?"

Donna huffed much like Fozzie when I can't keep up on our jogs. "Not Melody. Peyton's the one her grand-mother came to see. And who knows what the woman told her. She probably made me sound like some sort of wicked stepmother. No wonder Peyton doesn't want to have anything to do with me."

"Did this Harmony person actually tell you this?" Rox asked. "Because that's awfully specific."

"No." Donna folded her arms under her breasts, revealing an inch of cleavage at her ruffly V-neck. "But she made it pretty darn clear that Ian's concern for Peyton's welfare is overriding everything else in his life right now."

A single dad being protective of his only child wasn't a bad thing. "Honey, I think you're making too much out of this harbinger stuff. Just because—"

"No, just because you don't want to believe anything she told you doesn't mean that there wasn't a lot of truth in what she had to say," Donna said, raising her voice while Rox shot me a wary glance.

"You've always been so big on truth, so here's mine." Donna's gaze sharpened. "I love this guy. But I'm not going to say 'I do' until I know that we can make this marriage work. So I've made a decision, and I'm going to follow Harmony's advice whether you think I should or not."

I had yet to hear anything about this advice, so far be it for me to rain on Donna's mystery parade. "Okay. So what's the plan?"

"I haven't worked out all the details yet." She aimed a pink lacquered index finger at me. "But I'm gonna need your dog."

Huh?

Chapter Twenty-Four

I drove over to Tolliver's Funeral Home after work and did a slow roll past the parking lot to see if I recognized any of the cars.

Amongst the pickups and SUVs parked near the rear entrance, I spotted a red Corvette.

That meant that Trevor Constantine's funeral service was still underway. So I made a U-turn and parked under the shade of a giant Douglas fir, where I would have the most optimal street view of all the attendees as they filed out the door.

I didn't have to wait long for that door to open.

To my surprise, only one person exited the building— a shaggy-haired guy in a dark jacket and jeans, who jerked off his necktie as if it had been constricting his airway.

"Having trouble breathing there, Spencer?" Maybe because of a guilty conscience?

After Spencer Constantine peeled out of the parking lot in his beater pickup, his sister and parents emerged. While they exchanged hugs in front of one of the SUVs, another couple in black joined them.

I didn't recognize them. By the silver hair of the man, I guessed him to be close to Neil's age. Constantine family members from out of town, maybe?

The next couple who stepped out of the building required no guesswork. I recognized Brooke DeMatteo and her fiancé, Joel Stillwell, immediately. Same with Carlos holding the door for Paige and Amity.

The five of them stood by Carlos's Jeep and exchanged hugs while Leah and her parents didn't spare them so much as a glance, making it look like a dividing line in the parking lot had been drawn.

There was Team Farm Supply and Team Amity.

A family in black mourning attire versus a group of friends who had dressed as if they'd be clubbing later.

"Interesting fashion choice," I said, curious about the statement Amity was making in her form-fitting, off-the-shoulder cocktail dress. "I'm burying my husband. I'll wear whatever the heck I want?"

No matter her statement, her in-laws didn't answer back as they got into their vehicles and drove out of the parking lot in a three-car caravan with that other couple.

One of Amity's friends must have said something, because she turned to watch them leave.

I was too far away to take an accurate read of her body language, but the way Amity clung to Paige's side as Trevor's family drove away was heart-wrenching. It reminded me of how I felt seeing Chris's parents for the first time after he left me, like his decision had been my fault.

I thought I couldn't feel more wretched.

Then his mother fired me, proving me wrong.

"If that's what the dress is about, then good for you for looking fabulous in your wretchedness." It was way classier than the grease-stained chef's coat I'd tossed into the trash on my way out the door.

After one last squeezy hug, Paige and Carlos got into his Jeep and pulled out of the lot while Brooke, Joel, and Amity exchanged a few last words.

Finally, just the Corvette and Curtis Tolliver's old Saab remained in the lot, and after five minutes of watching Amity sit alone in her car, I wondered what she was waiting for.

Once another five minutes passed, the thought occurred to me that she had spotted me, and we were now playing a game of chicken.

Which one of us was going to be the first to make a move?

A loud rap on my passenger side window that made me about jump out of my skin answered that question.

And I was feeling especially chicken because Killian Havens was glaring at me through the glass.

"Unlock the door," he demanded.

Did he think I was stupid? "Actually, I was just leaving."

"You're going to explain what you're doing here first."

"I don't have to explain anything to you."

"Wrong answer. Now, unlock the door before I break it."

Crap. Crap. Crap.

Praying that I wasn't making a horrible mistake, I unlocked the passenger door.

"Okay," Killian said, folding himself into the bucket seat next to me. "Start talking."

"About what, exactly?"

A corner of his mouth curled with contempt, the gray eyes fixed on me as hard as granite. "About why I see you every time I turn around."

I tried to laugh him off, but I was so nervous little more than mousy squeaks came out. "I don't have to explain myself to you, especially since you were the one I discovered at the scene of a murder."

"I got there two minutes before you did."

"It was longer than that. I know because I was with your dad when he was looking for you."

"Okay, maybe three or four."

"A lot can happen in four minutes."

"Yeah, but I didn't do it."

"I didn't say that you did. It's just…"

"What?"

"You've been acting kind of guilty."

He vented a breath. "You don't even know me."

"I know, but ever since I first met you and Amity, I've been trying to make sense of all this."

"Well, stop trying, 'cause it's none of your business."

I saw movement behind him, and then a blonde with pink streaks glared at us through the window.

"What's going on?" Amity demanded.

"Nothing." The scowl he aimed at me suggested that it had better stay that way.

"Then what's she doing here?" Amity's volume was

increasing with every word that came out of her mouth.

"Exactly what I wanted to know," Killian said, opening the door.

The cool fresh air should have lowered the temperature inside my car, but the way these two were staring at me set my cheeks ablaze. "I was hoping to pay my respects, but when I saw the private service notice posted on the door, I decided to just offer up a prayer from here."

Just as I was doing now, with the hope that they would buy what I was trying to sell.

Killian shook his head. "Really? That's the best you can do?"

Yep. I had too much adrenaline pumping to conjure up anything more believable. "It's the truth."

"Well, the service is over so you can go home now," Amity stated with enough derision to inform me that she hadn't been any more impressed by my improvisation skills than her ex. "And Killian, we need to go."

He pointed a thick finger at me. "I don't want to see you hanging around anymore."

And I didn't want to find out what would happen if he did. "Understood."

"I haven't done anything wrong and neither has Amity."

Whoa! I believed him.

"So the next time I see you where you don't belong, I might not be so well-behaved." He leaned in to give me a hard stare that was probably intended to be menacing, but I could read that there was no bite behind his bark.

"Got it," I said, breathing a little easier.

"Kill! Come on! They're only going to stay open a few more minutes."

With Amity marching back across Tolliver's parking lot, Killian climbed out of my car and caught up with her after several long strides.

Seconds later, they disappeared through the door.

It almost looked normal. But a man and his ex-wife going inside to say their final good-byes to the man I had suspected them of murdering?

Not so normal.

Plus, half of that duo had just threatened me—an experience I didn't want to repeat anytime soon, so it was time to follow Amity's advice and go home.

At least I could leave with the certainty that Killian had told me the truth. That was a heck of a lot more than what I had arrived with.

It also left me with just one likely suspect: Spencer Constantine.

Chapter Twenty-Five

I spent most of Tuesday morning copying files that Shondra needed for a noon meeting. It probably should have been a two-hour job but expanded into three hours because the department's dinosaur of a copier kept overheating and shutting down like a temperamental toddler being given a time-out.

The copying also should have been done by one of her staffers yesterday. But he went home sick, and Shondra's administrative assistant didn't check his inbox until he didn't show up again this morning. That's when it became a *drop everything* emergency for me to do battle with the dinosaur.

Needless to say, there's nothing fun in such a battle. It does have one upside however: It creates goodwill.

And goodwill can create moments of opportunity—the very thing I was looking for when I headed to Shondra's office with my arms full with collated files.

"Knock, knock," I said, standing at her door.

Shondra pushed out of her desk chair. "Let me help you with those."

"They aren't that heavy. Where do you want them?"

She pointed at the round table in front of a three-shelf wall of books and knickknacks. "You can stack them there. The conference room won't be available for another few minutes."

I glanced back at the clock over her door. It was eleven-forty-two. "That's cutting it close for your meeting." Especially for me since I was the one responsible for prepping the room for each meeting on the schedule.

"Everything about this dang meeting has come together at the last minute. And before it gets any crazier and I forget to say it, I appreciate you helping out this morning."

How much? Because ... "I wanted to mention something to you, too."

Shondra sat back down behind her desk. "Please don't tell me that we need another copier again. It wasn't in the budget the last time you bitched to me about that beast, and it ain't in it now."

"We still need another copy machine, but that's not what I wanted to talk about because I discovered something that I need to report about Trevor Constantine's murder."

She narrowed her eyes. "*You* discovered something."

I nodded.

"In an active criminal investigation that shouldn't require any inquiries made by one of this department's deputies because it's being handled by an experienced and highly respected sheriff's detective?"

Well, when she put it that way. "I didn't do anything in an official capacity. I just happened to be in the right place at the right time to talk to Killian Havens."

Shondra hung her head and groaned. "Lord, help me if you asked him if he did it. Because if you caught him in a lie—"

"No! That's just it. He didn't lie. He told the truth when he said that the only reason he went to the Constantines' house that morning was because of the barking dog. Same as me."

She looked up. "That's it?"

"So I'm convinced that he and Amity Constantine had nothing to do with the murder."

"Good for you. You won't mind, though, if Detective Pearson continues with his investigation and comes to his own conclusions."

"I'm not trying to—"

"Girl, I know exactly what you're trying to do," Shondra said, leaning back in her chair. "And I know your intentions are good, but I don't need to remind you that you're a witness, so don't strike up any more conversations with anyone connected to this investigation."

"That's not exactly what I was trying to do."

"I don't care. You need to walk away. Preferably in the direction of that conference room because they should be out of there by now."

I still needed to tell her what I knew about Spencer Constantine. "But you should know that—"

"Let it go, Charmaine."

If someone said that to me one more time, I was going to scream.

✳

Like my least favorite copy machine, I needed some time to cool off and thought I'd head to the waterfront and grab a sandwich. But first, I had to make it past Patsy, who was crooking her finger at me.

"Going out to lunch?" she asked.

I knew I didn't have to worry about her wanting to join me. Patsy had made it clear from my first day working in the department that she and I wouldn't become lunch buddies.

That didn't mean that I shouldn't play nice with the guard dog outside Frankie's office. "Want me to bring something back for you?"

"No." Patsy lowered her head, affording me an excellent view of her gray roots as she picked up the small cardboard box at her feet. "This needs to be delivered. The attorney's address is on the envelope."

Patsy handed me the box that appeared to contain copies of the files that I had made for the head of the criminal division yesterday. Reading the address, I saw that my destination would be a Gibson Lake law office.

Gibson Lake was a former fishing destination of my grandfather's, located out on Route 104 at the western boundary of the county. It would take almost an hour to get there and an hour back, longer with a stop for lunch.

Fortunately, I didn't have any afternoon meetings I needed to rush back to, because it just so happened that I had some unfinished business with a widow who lived along the way.

Chapter Twenty-Six

Thirty minutes later, I called my mother while rolling to a stop in front of Amity Constantine's farm house.

"Charmaine, you have excellent timing," Marietta chirped. "Because I was just about to call you."

Uh-oh. "What for?"

"I need you to help me edit that video."

"What video?"

"The one you shot of me, silly girl."

"I don't know how to edit cell phone video."

"Barry has some app on his laptop. He says it's easy to use."

"Then have him do it."

"I can't very well do that. I want it to be a surprise for his birthday."

This was so not what I wanted to talk to her about. "Fine. We'll see if we can figure it out together. Not today, but later in the week."

"Wonderful! Can we make it Thursday? Barry is having an early birthday dinner in Seattle with his son, so I'm sure he won't get back until late."

"Thursday works for me." I looked up to see Amity

glaring at me from her porch while she held back Max. "I can't talk much longer. I just called to find out what headshot you want me to give Amity."

"The one I use for all my public appearances," my mother said, using a tone that suggested that I should have known that she intended to keep trotting out her old Hollywood glamour shot for the next twenty years.

"Got it. Thanks."

I disconnected and scrambled out of my car to give Amity a friendly wave. "Hi. I was in the area on business and thought this might be a good opportunity to provide you with Marietta's headshot. You still plan on producing some flyers for the spa's grand opening, right? Or should I be talking to Brooke about this?"

"No, she doesn't have time, so Paige and I are creating the flyers." Amity's eyes were guarded, and after the last week I couldn't blame her. "As for your mom's picture, you could have emailed it to me."

"Yes, but I was hoping to talk to you for a few minutes."

She heaved a sigh. "What now?"

Amity disappeared inside the house with Max trotting at her feet. With the door left open, I assumed that was my cue to explain myself.

"First, I wanted to apologize for yesterday," I said, taking the chair to her left, just like the last time I was in her living room. "I didn't mean to intrude."

"And yet that's exactly what you keep doing."

Fair enough. "I had the wrong idea about your ex-husband's involvement..."

The flash of anger igniting her cheeks told me that I needed to change the subject. "Anyway, I'm sorry."

She stroked the head of the dog lying next to her. "And I'm sorry if Killian scared you yesterday. He's not a bad guy. He's just not great with people."

I had noticed. "I get that. He seemed to be sneaking around when I first saw him on your porch, so he and I didn't get off to the best start."

"I didn't help the situation when I thought that he..." Amity swiped at the tears trickling down her cheeks. "When I came home, I thought something must have gone horribly wrong... and Killian... I accused him..."

Shaking her head, she ducked around the corner with Max following her, and then emerged, wiping her face with a wad of tissue. "Anyway, I should have known that he couldn't hurt Trev."

"I know they were close once," I said, crossing the room so that I could better see her.

Amity teared up again. "I'm afraid I ruined that."

"I'm sure it wasn't your fault." Okay, *entirely* her fault.

"No one around here would believe me, but I was trying to make things better. I thought..." Amity pressed the tissues against her leaky eyes. "That once Killian left, it would be okay."

She was losing me. "Killian was leaving?" Was this what he had confided to his mother? That he wasn't leaving alone? "You mean with Max?"

Amity nodded. "He wasn't even supposed to be here."

What? "He who?"

"Trevor," she gasped between sniffs.

"Your husband wasn't supposed to be home when he was killed?"

Amity shook her head.

"Where was he supposed to be?"

"The gym. He went every Sunday around noon, and then he was going to the cemetery to take his mom some flowers."

If Trevor made a habit out of going to the gym on Sundays, a lot of people around here would have known his schedule.

"So are you saying that Killian was supposed to come over here to get Max after Trevor left? And then what? Drive back to Alaska?"

"That was the plan." Amity wrapped her arms around Max like she needed something to hold onto. "Trevor loved this guy as much as I do, and would have never agreed to let Killian take him home. But I thought it was the easiest solution to give everybody what they wanted. Trevor and I could sell this place and move somewhere that doesn't stink like cow." Burying her face in Max's rough coat, her shoulders heaved. "When I said good-bye to Killian and drove away, I thought everything was gonna be fine."

Maybe it would have been. If someone else hadn't come along.

※

The clock tower chimed twice as I climbed the marble

steps of the courthouse and met the steely gaze of the sheriff's deputy with the buzz cut working security while court was in session.

But I was much more interested in the blue-eyed brunette who was looking at me from where she sat alone on the same wooden bench where I had seen her mother five days earlier.

"What are you doing here?" Brooke DeMatteo asked after I gave her a little wave.

I closed the distance between us so that I could keep our volume low and avoid getting shushed by the deputy. "I work in the building." I didn't want her to think that I had anything to do with the prosecution of her mother, so I didn't mention which department.

"Are you here waiting for someone?" Because if Brooke was waiting to see her mother, it could be another hour before Judge Witten adjourned for the day.

She uncrossed her long legs, shifting uncomfortably in her seat. "To testify. I'm being called as a witness."

"You witnessed a crime or something?" I asked to get a glimpse at how much Brooke knew about what her mother had been up to.

"No, that's just it. There was no crime. It's all a big misunderstanding."

I had complete trust in Frankie, that she wouldn't have brought the case against Barbara DeMatteo if there hadn't been rock-solid evidence to get a conviction. But as convinced as I was of that fact, I could see that Brooke believed every word that had just come out of her mouth.

That would make Brooke a compelling witness for the defense, but it made me wonder if she had been so absorbed by the events in her own life that she had tunnel vision when it came to her mother.

It also made me very aware that the courtroom door could open any second, and I didn't want to be seen talking to a witness prior to giving her testimony.

"Then I'm sure it'll be fine," I said with a bright smile while she fiddled with the bowtie of her plum polyester blouse.

Lisa is going to rip you and your little bowtie apart on cross-examination.

Brooke nodded. "That's what I keep telling myself, but lately... It's just been a lot."

A friend murdered and her mother standing trial while Brooke and Joel Stillwell feverishly labored to reopen their day spa? Yep, that was the textbook definition of "a lot."

She brightened. "At least this trial will be over soon so everything can get back to normal."

With her mother facing an almost certain prison sentence? *Good luck with that.*

"Well, I should get back to work," I said, inching away from her before that door opened.

"See you at the grand opening." Brooke handed me a card from her tote bag. "This is good for ten percent off any treatment that day, so be sure to come."

"I'll be there with my mother."

"Great! Here's one for your mom," she said, giving me another card.

She obviously didn't understand why I'd be accompanying my mother. "She's Marietta Moreau and doesn't need a discount card since—"

"Oh! I didn't realize you two were related." Brooke snatched back the card. "No, your mom won't need the discount. Everything will be on the house for our celebrity guest."

"She's looking forward to it." I said with my feet in motion. "I gave Amity Marietta's headshot, but if there's anything else you need from us prior to the grand opening, don't hesitate to ask."

When the courtroom door creaked open and the bailiff called her name, Brooke waved at me like a beauty queen in a parade. "Awesome."

Yeah, awesomely oblivious.

Not so awesome, the way the bailiff was scowling at me so I scurried into the prosecutor's office, where I discovered Steve sitting in the lobby staring at his cell phone.

"Don't suppose you've been waiting for me," I said, giving his foot a playful tap.

"Nope." Steve looked me up and down, and smiled as if he liked what he saw. "I've got a meeting with Ben."

Ben was the head of the criminal division so there was nothing unusual about them meeting, especially when charges were about to be filed.

"This wouldn't have anything to do with Trevor—"

"No." Steve pocketed his phone. "And beyond that, no comment."

"Because you can't provide any commentary or because you don't have any new news?"

"Yes."

"I do love our talks. You can be so engaging."

His lips curled into a sexy grin. "I'd like to engage on a certain topic with you later."

"Oh yeah? Well, maybe I won't be the one in the mood to talk."

"Who said anything about talking?" Steve whispered in my ear as Ben called his name from the hallway.

"Do I at least get a dinner out of this non-talking date?"

Steve looked back over his shoulder. "It would be my pleasure to provide you dinner and anything else you might desire."

Goody.

Chapter Twenty-Seven

After falling asleep in Steve's arms, I woke around one, and then headed home, where I spent the next four hours replaying Amity's words as if they were on a continuous loop in my head.

A jog around the park with Fozzie in the crisp pre-dawn air failed to clear my head. Instead, with each foot-fall, I felt like I was pounding away on the same question that had been consuming me for over a week: Who killed Trevor Constantine?

I had no answers. I didn't even have any bright ideas, so I showered and changed, and headed over to Duke's to find out if Alice or Lucille had anything illuminating.

"What do you mean, she didn't have anything to do with her husband's murder?" Alice demanded within five minutes of me joining her at her worktable. "The girl stands to make a bundle and everyone knows she only married Trevor for his money."

It sounded like my great-aunt was quoting Dorothy Constantine again. "I talked to Amity. She didn't do it, and before you say anything, Killian didn't do it either."

"Okay, smartypants, then who did?"

"I'm with Lucille that it might have been Spencer."

"About time someone around here sees it my way," she announced, pouring fresh brew into our cups. "What I can't understand is why they haven't already arrested that kid."

That "kid" was probably only a couple of years younger than me. "If there are no witnesses that can place him there, and with no evidence…"

"Yeah, yeah." Lucille slid onto the wooden stool next to Alice. "I watch *Law and Order*. I know what it takes to make charges stick. It's just frustrating is all."

Tell me about it.

"You know what's frustrating?" Duke barked as he lumbered in our direction. "Having people on my payroll playing hide and seek with the coffee."

Lucille smiled saccharine-sweet as she filled the cup in his hand. "Two of those people knew exactly where it is."

He glared at me. "And the third keeps showing up and distracting them while they're supposed to be working."

"Are you insinuating that I'm not working?" Alice cocked her head at him.

"You're looking at a man who doesn't have a death wish, so no, dear."

She flicked her wrist to shoo him away. "Enough said, then."

"Is it too much to ask to have a nice, normal day around here?" he grumbled, heading back to prep his grill for opening.

I stared into the muddy depths of my coffee cup.

"Normal would be good." But it felt like that day was somewhere on a distant horizon given everything that had happened since I took Gram to that Mother's Day brunch.

"Ignore him. We do," Lucille said with a rheumy chuckle. "And we're glad to see you, 'cause we need to talk."

Alice gave her old pal a dark glance. "Luce, this better not be about what I think it is."

That didn't sound good. "What's going on?"

"You tell us." Lucille's eyes held a predatory gleam as she planted her elbows in flour dust. "Because I heard a rumor that you went to see a psychic."

Crappity, crap, crap, crap!

Donna had known that I didn't want our visit to Harmony House to become public knowledge. Why would she say anything about it?

"A psychic?" I aimed my best withering stare across the table. "Give me a break."

Lucille's tangerine-painted lips curved with amusement. "That's not a denial."

"Then it's true?" Alice's eyes widened behind her wire-rimmed trifocals. "Miriam was right?"

I didn't know what Miriam had to do with this, other than the fact that she was one of Lucille's main gossip suppliers. "I...uh..."

"I knew it!" Lucille exclaimed. "The moment that Miriam told me that Carmen told her all about the psychic that Donna and a friend went to, I figured that friend had to be you."

"Donna has lots of friends." And Carmen and Miriam had big mouths.

"But there's only one I can think of who would want a psychic to tell her about the murder that happened next door." Lucille reached for her cup. "Don't hear you denyin' that either."

I swore under my breath. "You could get me into a lot of trouble at work if either of you repeat any of what you *think* you know to anyone else."

Alice's mouth gaped open. "Then it's true."

"I told ya." Lucille scooted closer. "So what'd the psychic have to say? Did she provide you with some sort of description of the murderer?"

I shushed her. "No, and again, this can't be repeated to any—"

"We know." Lucille waved her hand impatiently. "We're sworn to secrecy. Now, give. What'd she tell you?"

"Not a whole lot." At least nothing I felt like I could admit to. "I was more interested if she had seen or heard anything around the time of the murder."

"And?" Lucille asked.

"She didn't." I didn't mention Clio and had no intention of providing Lucille anything meaty for her to chew on.

Lucille blinked. "Nothing at all?"

I shook my head. "She wasn't even home at the time."

"Well, that's disappointing, but if she's any kind of psychic at all, she should have picked up some sort of vibration that the dude was in trouble, and then rushed home so that she could help ID the killer."

That would have been convenient. "That doesn't seem to be how it works for her."

Alice leaned in. "Then how does it work?"

"She holds objects belonging to the person and interprets cards. And is probably pretty skilled when it comes to picking up cues from her clients." I looked across the table at Lucille. "But she couldn't tell me anything about who killed Trevor Constantine that I didn't already know."

Lucille frowned. "Then she's a piss-poor excuse for a psychic."

"What exactly did she say?" Alice asked.

"You know. General stuff like he was angry and got caught up in a situation." And other more personal stuff I didn't want to discuss.

"Who was angry?" Alice leaned closer. "The killer?"

I nodded.

"Well, duh!" Lucille glowered at me. "Of course he was angry. Who stabs somebody 'cause they're in a good mood?"

"Which was pretty much what I thought, but Donna had fun, so..." I hoped that would be enough to satisfy their curiosity.

"If it's a 'he' that eliminates Amity, though," Alice said. "And I was so sure about her. Of course, it could still be a murder for hire kind of thing."

"I've eliminated her as a suspect. Killian, too. Whatever was going on with them prior to the murder wasn't what a lot of people thought." Including me.

"That leaves Spencer." Lucille slapped the tabletop, raising a plume of flour dust. "I knew it was him."

"Or Neil." Alice turned to Lucille. "I haven't wanted to consider the possibility, but after hearing about how tempers were flaring at that family meeting, well... How can we leave him off our suspect list?"

Lucille shrugged. "Neil's no hot head. I still think it's Spencer."

"It's six o'clock," Duke bellowed. "So I think it's time to cut the chatter and get to work."

"Yeah, yeah. I'm coming." Lucille got to her feet. "Don't get your knickers into a twist."

"Remember," I said to her as she stood over me. "You can't repeat anything we talked about."

"Don't you get your knickers into a twist neither. I swear, you worry too much about what other people say."

Only because I didn't want to be featured as the gossip topic du jour.

Once Lucille squeaked away, I looked across the table at my great-aunt Alice. "That goes for you too. You can't repeat any of this to anyone because I don't want it getting back to Gram."

Alice cast a worried glance at her half-filled muffin tin. "That could present a problem, 'cause your grandmother and I talked last night."

I buried my head in my hands. "You didn't."

"I didn't know that it was supposed to be a big secret. We talked about the fortune teller that Mary Jo dragged your granny to back before you were born. How she said your mom was gonna be rich and famous someday."

Which turned out to be true for a brief time.

"Anyway, I don't think you have anything to worry about there," Alice assured me. "Eleanor will probably just want to hear about the highlights of your visit, and that will be that."

That couldn't be that, especially with Steve coming over for dinner.

Almost twelve hours later, I rushed to my grand-mother's house so that I could have a few minutes alone with her before Steve showed up for tonight's lasagna dinner.

"So you can understand why Donna thought it would be interesting to go," I reiterated, having emphasized the fact that Harmony Peel was something of a psychic counselor. "But she and I haven't even shared everything that happened during our sessions, so despite Aunt Alice blabbing to a few people about this, I need to ask you to respect Donna's privacy. Mine too, because I really don't want Steve to know about this."

Gram looked up from the table she had been setting and planted her hands on her ample hips. "Okay. What aren't you telling me?"

"That's pretty much it." It had to be.

"Uh-huh. I'll have you know that you're not the only one in this house who can tell when someone's lying."

"Gram—"

"Yep, you're trying to keep something from me and

Stevie. What in the world did that woman tell you?"

"Nothing."

"Then what's so horrible about what you and Donna did that you don't want anyone to know about it?"

"Nothing!" Much. "It's just that the place is located on the other side of the fence from Constantine's and—"

"Oh, I get it. Someone there witnessed the murder."

"No! I was hoping that they might have seen something, but it ended up being a waste of time."

"Then why are you making a big deal out of this?"

"Because I don't want Steve thinking that I'm getting overly involved in the investigation."

She looked at me over her glasses. "Well..."

"Don't say it. I already know not to take this any further."

"Good. I don't want to worry about you. I'm sure Stevie doesn't want to either. Oh, and as long as we're on the subject of the man in your life, what did Madame What's-her-name have to say about him?"

"I didn't ask any questions about him."

"Really? No love-life stuff? How disappointing."

"She mentioned an S-name, but didn't say much of anything worth repeating. So please don't you say anything. I don't want Steve to think that I'm talking to strangers about him... about us." About a relationship I had a hard time putting words to for fear that I would jinx it.

Smiling, Gram patted my cheek. "I know exactly what you mean, but I don't think you have anything to worry about where he's concerned."

Says you. "I still don't want you saying anything about it. Not with him, not with Mom, not with anybody."

"Oh." Gram's smile twisted into a grimace. "That could be a problem."

"Please don't tell me..."

"Your mother called earlier, and we got to talking."

I groaned.

"I obviously didn't have any details to share with her, so your mom's looking forward to hearing all about it when you go over there tomorrow."

I stared at my grandmother in disbelief.

"Oh, come on," she protested. "She's family. We don't keep secrets from family."

Yes, we do!

Chapter Twenty-Eight

"What do you mean it's a privacy thing?" Marietta demanded after I recited the sixty-second version of the story I had concocted a day earlier for my grandmother.

I looked up from the laptop that Barry had left running on their kitchen table for me. "You of all people should understand the concept of privacy, as in this is my personal business. So I'd appreciate it if you'd not mention it to anyone, especially Steve."

"Why would you want to keep this from Steve? Unless…" Her eyes lit up as her mouth formed a perfect oval. "It's because she talked about the two of you getting married, isn't it?"

Good grief. "The subject barely came up."

My mother abandoned the lettuce she had been chopping and clapped with glee. "He's going to propose! I knew it was just a matter of time."

"He hasn't proposed, so let's not go crazy and read stuff into this that isn't there. Because what she said was that she saw a wedding in my future."

"Like I said, just a matter of time. Ooh, we should start looking for dresses!"

I stared up at her. "I have a dress—a *bridesmaid* dress for Donna's wedding, the only wedding that's in my immediate future."

Disappointment pulled at Marietta's Cupid's bow lips. "Honestly, Charmaine. If I didn't know better, I'd think that you didn't want to get married again."

"Unlike you, I haven't wanted to rush into something," I muttered under my breath.

"What was that?" Picking up her knife, she aimed a parental look at me that left no doubt that I should choose my next words carefully.

"I said I don't want to rush into anything."

"I don't think that's quite what you said, but that's okay. Because I absolutely agree."

She did?

Then why did she keep bringing up the subject?

"There's no reason to rush," Marietta added with a shake of her head. "You're barely thirty-five."

"Thirty-six next month." Not that I was in any more of a hurry to admit to it than she was.

"Still, my point is that you two have plenty of time."

That sounded like a reference to my biological clock—something that I didn't want to hear or think about, so instead, I focused on uploading the video recording from my phone.

"And while I completely understand that you've wanted to take it slow, as your mama, I do feel obligated to say that I don't want you to be *afraid* to get married again."

I could barely keep a lid on the primal scream bubbling up from my gut. "Can we stop talking about this, please?"

"I'm just sayin' that the past doesn't equal the future. Steve isn't Chris, and I know he loves you, so don't let the old hurts from the past hold you back."

Criminy, she was echoing what Harmony told me. "Great advice. Thanks, Mom."

Pulling a rotisserie chicken from her refrigerator, Marietta heaved a sigh. "Fine. I'll say no more on the subject, but we should still go shopping. Do you need shoes to go with your dress? Maybe we could go to Port Townsend after we're done at the spa."

Swell. A full day of togetherness.

"Maybe," I said, watching my cell phone video on Barry's laptop.

"While we're there we could stop in at that cute bridal shop we went to for your dress for my wedding."

Now it was my turn to heave a sigh. "I thought we had put the subject of wedding dress shopping to bed."

"Well, one of us may have."

"It's time for you to think about something else, so come over here and tell me what you want to do with this video."

"Oh, how fun," Marietta said, pulling over a chair to sit next to me.

While she donned the reading glasses she'd left near the laptop, I angled it to give her the best view of the screen. "It's a little over two minutes long, so we might want to edit it down."

"Let's just see what we have first." Her fingers hovered over the keyboard. "Is there a play button on this thing?"

I clicked play with the touchpad, and leaned back to finally take a sip of the rosé she had poured when I arrived fifteen minutes earlier.

Gasping, she swatted at my leg. "Good lord, why didn't you tell me that I laughed like a hyena?"

Because our relationship was on shaky enough ground. "You sound like you're having a good time. It's fine."

"It's *not* fine! That will have to be edited."

I turned down the volume. "You can narrate over the parts you don't like."

"So far, it's the whole thing." She muttered her favorite swear word in rapid succession. "No wonder no one wants to hire me. I look and sound ridiculous."

"No, you don't." Maybe a little.

She cringed when Neil Constantine had to jump out of her way.

"We'll definitely want to cut that part out," I said. "It's a good thing you turned when you did. You were heading right for Amity's house."

Slumping, Marietta folded her arms under her double Ds at the same time that I saw movement at Amity's kitchen window. "I missed it, didn't I?"

"Wait a second. Let's see that again." I paused the video and pulled the laptop close to get a better look.

"So I got a teensy bit close to her house. You don't have to make a big deal out of it. In fact, let's forget the whole thing and pretend it never happened."

"Okay, but let me check something first," I said, clicking on the slider bar to replay the last ten seconds. "I thought I saw something."

She straightened, pushing her glasses up her nose. "What? Where?"

I pointed at the window and then pressed play. "Watch the curtain. Someone pulls it back."

"Who is that?" she asked, her nose inches away from the screen. "I don't think I've seen him before. Do you recognize him?"

"Yep." Because it was Rory Havens.

"You're absolutely sure it was Rory and not Killian?" Gram asked while I helped myself to a slab of leftover lasagna.

I had become well-acquainted with Killian's scowl over the last week and a half. This wasn't that. In fact, Rory had looked mildly amused, probably because of how high Neil Constantine had jumped in his effort to keep all his toes. "It was him, all right."

"That's very odd. From the way Gaylene talked about their former daughter-in-law being a thorn in their collective sides, it's hard to imagine Rory making a social call."

"That's what I thought," I said, popping my plate into her microwave.

Gram frowned. "What are you doing? Didn't you just eat over at your mother's?"

"She made a chicken salad with not enough chicken

and not enough salad. Plus, it had a funky dressing."

"She tries."

"Yes, she does." And tried my patience more often than not. "You've known Rory Havens for a long time. Tell me why he would play hooky on a Saturday afternoon—probably the busiest time of his work week—to pay a visit to his son's ex-wife."

Gram eased into her usual chair at the kitchen table. "He must've had a good reason to leave Killian minding the garden center by himself."

"It wouldn't be to offer his condolences," I said, carrying my plate to the table. "Because he could have done that anytime."

"Maybe Rory went over there to talk to Amity about all the time his son had been spending with her. Gaylene could've asked him to do it. That's a possibility if they thought Amity was stringing Killian along."

"Maybe."

"I can't imagine him doing that during peak business hours, though. It had to have been a more time-sensitive matter."

While I chewed on a cheesy bite of lasagna, my brain gnawed on the most important time-sensitive matter that would have existed last weekend. "Like the investigation."

"That sure seems more likely. Especially if Rory thought that Killian could have gotten himself tangled up in something."

I couldn't help but smile. "You're referring to your 'cahoots' theory."

"I'm not the only one who thought there might be something to that."

"I know, and it wasn't a bad theory. But I was there when Mr. Havens saw Killian coming back with the dog. There wasn't any blood on him, and he seemed pretty calm. So Mr. Havens shouldn't have had any reason to think that Killian was up to anything, other than being sneaky about getting his dog back."

"Then what was Rory doing at that gal's house in the middle of the day?"

"I wish I knew."

Gram gave me a worried glance. "You don't think he had anything to do with the murder, do you?"

"I didn't before seeing him at that window."

"He would have had to give an account of his time. Just like you did when you were questioned by Jim Pearson, right?"

"Sure," I said with my mouth full.

"Wait a minute. There's no way that Rory did it. When I first went to check out his tomatoes, there he was by the greenhouse, washing his hands with his hose. Heck, if it came to it, I could provide him an alibi."

I almost choked on my last bite of lasagna. "You saw him washing his hands?" *Probably mere minutes after the time of the murder?*

Gram nodded. "And his boots. I assumed he got muddy out in the berry fields."

Or bloody just past the berry fields.

Chapter Twenty-Nine

My biggest issue with working with fourteen coffee-guzzling, paper-producing, ego-driven attorneys was that most of them seemed to be allergic to the concept of cleaning up after themselves.

The courthouse had a maintenance staff to clean the floors and dispose of the trash. But no one wanted to touch the breakroom refrigerator, especially after some junior prosecutor's lunch had devolved into looking like a science experiment. So once a month, Patsy would post a reminder on the breakroom door to label anything you wanted to keep, otherwise it would be disposed of.

Specifically by me.

I would take a half hour in the middle of what was usually a slow Friday afternoon to empty the refrigerator and then scour it with disinfectant just like I had last month and the many months before that.

Most of the time no one complained about me cleaning up after them like a fairy godmother.

This particular Friday wasn't one of those times. Because the second that I gathered up the plastic trash bag with several rank containers of unknown origin, Lisa

Arbuckle swung open the refrigerator door and then glared at the bag in my hand as if I were making off with her lunch.

"Where's my cake?" the petite blonde demanded.

I had a bad feeling about the white bakery sack from Duke's at the bottom of my trash bag. "Was your name on it?"

"It was a slice of cake. I had only put it in there this morning."

I gave her my best customer service smile, the one I used to reserve for the surliest of the kitchen czars I had worked for. "If your name was on it, it would still be there."

With a dark stare that could freeze Merritt Bay, she stepped toward me, straightening to almost eye-level in her three-inch pumps. "I was needed in court."

Even though Lisa couldn't have weighed more than a hundred and ten in her pantsuit and pearls, I'd often seen her use her physicality to break down the defenses of witnesses.

But they were typically sitting down to give her a height advantage.

And they weren't there to testify to what they knew about a stupid piece of cake.

"The jury had just come back," she added as if I needed a reminder of our power dynamic.

I didn't need to be put in my place. I was well aware, and felt no compulsion to apologize for doing my job. "The DeMatteo case?"

A prideful smile twitched at Lisa's lips. "A conviction

on five counts."

"Congratulations." I couldn't help but think of Brooke. She had been in such denial about the dire straits her mother was in. And now…

Actually, I wasn't sure what would happen next. "Will she go to prison?"

"Sentencing will be in about thirty days, but yes. She'll get at least a year and will be ordered to pay restitution."

Based on how much Barbara had skimmed from the construction company over the ten years she had worked there, I imagined that could cost Barbara her home.

"What happens in the meantime?"

Lisa gave me the same pained look I used to get from Marietta when I'd ask too many questions about my sperm-donor father. "She's not much of a flight risk so she gets to enjoy her freedom for a little while longer."

"Good. Because her daughter's got a grand opening thing going on next weekend. Not that it matters with everything else going on, but she probably expects Barbara to be there."

"Yeah, Brooke mentioned that when she was testifying."

"Really." Then she was even more clueless than I had thought. "Probably not what the defense attorney wanted her to talk about."

"But the more she talked, the more she showed how little she knew about where some of the money she got to buy that spa had come from." Lisa stepped in front of the coffeemaker. "Brooke was kept in the dark by design.

The mom sheltering her daughter from the harsh reality of what she'd done." She gave me a long look after she took the last of the coffee. "But there comes a time when we must accept the situation that we find ourselves in, whether we want to or not."

The snark in her tone told me we weren't talking about the DeMatteos anymore.

Lisa smiled, waiting while she sugared her coffee.

Clearly, that was my cue to consider my situation.

"I need to run to the post office in a few minutes." I didn't, but everything about her body language screamed that she didn't care what I said as long as it came out in an ingratiating manner. "Why don't I pick you up a piece of cake while I'm out."

"Would you? Gee, that'd be swell." Dropping the smile as if she were done with me, Lisa marched to the door in her chunky heels. "I'd prefer carrot cake, but white cake with raspberry filling is a good second choice. And a latte with a pump of vanilla. Actually, make it two pumps. I'm celebrating."

She disappeared into the hallway, leaving me holding a stinky sack of garbage and no money to pay for her celebration.

Some days I hated being a fairy godmother.

Fifteen minutes later, I returned the remaining five slices of carrot cake to the bakery display case and grabbed a chocolate chip cookie for my trouble as well as a balm for my foul mood.

"That ain't a free buffet," Duke announced from be-hind the grill while I stood at the cash register and watched the pies rotate by. "Drop a contribution in there and get back to work."

"You should be nicer to your customers or they won't want to come back."

"I'm plenty nice," he deadpanned while flipping a burger. "To the paying ones."

I waved several dollar bills at him prior to ringing up my tab. "Happy?"

"Delirious."

"Where is everyone?" I asked when I made a scan of the sparsely populated diner and spotted only Courtney working the four occupied tables.

"I dunno. At work? Since lunch break should have ended over an hour ago."

"In case you're trying to tell me something." In a not-so-subtle way. "I *am* working." I held up the white bakery bag in my hand. "This is for one of the attorneys I work for."

"You're fetching them dessert now? That's some 'spe-cial assistant' job you've got."

"Yeah well, some days are more special than others."

I peeked past him to see Alice's work space looking conspicuously tidy. "Where's your wife?"

"You just missed her. It's mahjong night with your granny, so she hitched a ride home with Luce." Duke slanted me a glance as he plated the burger. "Why?"

"As long as I was here, I thought I'd ask her opinion about something."

"I got opinions."

"I've noticed." But I didn't think he'd know as much about Rory Havens as Aunt Alice would.

"Order up!" he called out, setting the plate on the shiny aluminum counter in front of him. "So what's on your mind?"

With Courtney approaching I hesitated to say anything about one of Duke's produce suppliers, so I waved at her instead of answering.

"Hey, Char," Courtney said with a friendly smile while Duke wiped his hands on a kitchen rag.

"Well?" Slinging the rag over his shoulder, he knitted his bushy silver eyebrows. "You wanna talk to me or not?"

"Not here." I pulled him back toward his doughnut fryer. "Rory Havens is someone you've done business with for a while, right?"

"Yeah," Duke said, wariness creeping into his gaze.

"Have you ever seen him angry?"

"Can't say that I have." He folded his beefy arms. "What's this about, exactly?"

"I've only met the guy a couple of times and am trying to get a sense of the type of person he is."

"Why?"

I didn't want to answer that question. "Never mind why."

"You said you wanted an opinion about something. This sounds more like you want some dirt on the guy."

That's exactly what I wanted. "Okay, let me rephrase my question. In your opinion, is Rory Havens capable of getting physical with somebody, say if he's provoked?"

"I am, so I guess he would be too."

"Yeah, you're so tough."

"Don't you forget it, baby girl. So, is that it? You just want to know if Rory can handle himself?"

"More or less."

"Did something happen I don't know about?"

Yep. "Like I said, I'm just trying to get a sense of the guy."

"Oh, I get it. It's because of what happened to that Constantine kid, isn't it?"

"Uh… I'm not at liberty to say."

"'Not at liberty to say.'" He loomed over me. "That's because you're still pokin' your nose where it doesn't belong."

"I'm just trying to make sense of something having to do with Mr. Havens."

"I have an opinion on the best way for you to do that. You wanna hear it?"

It didn't sound like I had much choice in the matter. "Sure."

"Go back to work, do your job, and keep your nose clean."

"Very helpful advice. Thanks a lot," I grumbled as I left the kitchen.

"Any time, kiddo. There's more where that came from."

Of that I had no doubt. I just wished I felt the same certainty about Rory Havens.

Chapter Thirty

After a quick trip home to feed Fozzie and change so that I wouldn't smell like disinfectant, I arrived at Eddie's where the typical Friday night crowd had assembled at the bar.

Unfortunately, that crowd didn't include my date.

They also hadn't left me a seat, so I came around to the end of the bar, where Rox was waiting for me with a bottle of chardonnay.

"The usual, madam?" she asked with a bright smile.

I didn't know what I was in the mood for besides some fun distraction from Steve. And cookies. Preferably warm and gooey.

In lieu of warm and gooey, cool and alcoholic would have to suffice. "That's fine."

Having received an earlier text from Donna that she and Ian would meet us here after he finished at the clinic, I scanned the room and noticed a pretty girl in a black Eddie's Place T-shirt delivering two pizzas to a group near the entrance.

With the way several heads swiveled when the dark-haired beauty zipped by in a tight pair of blue jeans, I wasn't the only one. "Looks like you found some help."

"We did, and thank goodness for that, 'cause I was getting desperate," Rox said while she poured. "Her name's Sofia. Used to work at a bar in Port Townsend, but this is closer to home for her. So far, she's working out great and is a big hit with the guys."

"I noticed. How about you? Need any help tonight?"

"Relax. Eddie will be taking over here in a few, so we've got it covered."

That should have come as good news, but I found it as annoying as the Olivia Newton-John mellow schmaltz in my ear. "Great," I said on a sigh.

"What's with the sigh? Are you incapable of enjoying a night off?"

"Sorry. It's been a long, weird week."

"Tell Mama."

"I just feel… I don't know. Useless."

"What do you mean? At work?"

I nodded. "Want to hear about the most important thing that I accomplished today? I cleaned out a disgusting refrigerator."

"At least you got paid for it. I got puked on twice this morning by a demon baby. So when it comes to who had the more disgusting day, I win."

"He won't always be a demon baby."

"Promise?" Eddie interjected as he slid past me to join Rox behind the bar.

"If you want a sitter so you can have a little down time, I'm available this weekend." Because I sure wasn't accomplishing anything else worthwhile in my spare time.

"Thanks." Rox smiled back over her shoulder as she headed over to the register with Eddie. "But I wouldn't wish the little milk monster on anyone right now. Besides, something tells me you're gonna be busy."

Huh? "What do you know that I don't know?"

"She knows that you're gonna be helping me tomorrow," Donna said, hugging me from behind.

Turning, I saw that she was alone. "Where's Ian? He's still coming, right?" Because if he had cancelled again and Donna expected me to make a repeat appearance at his clinic with Fozzie...

"He'll be here around six-thirty, which doesn't give us much time. When's Steve getting here?"

"Don't know. I assume he's running late."

"Good." Donna's long hair spilled over her shoulders as she squeezed by to snatch up my wineglass, and I caught a whiff of her pear-scented shampoo.

"What exactly is going on?"

Instead of answering, Donna signaled to Rox that she wanted a glass for herself and then made tracks toward an empty table along the back wall. "Come with me."

"I hope you're gonna tell me that things are better between you and Ian," I said when we sat across from one another at the table for four. "It's been a rotten little day and I could really use some good news."

Joy lit up Donna's creamy cheeks as she pushed my drink toward me. "It's all good. Ian finally opened up and told me what happened."

"That is good." And about time.

Donna nodded. "I won't bore you with all the details, but that harbinger of darkness stuff that Harmony talked about, that was his former mother-in-law, all right. She said some stuff to Peyton—probably unintentional—but it made the poor little thing scared about the wedding, about leaving Winnie and moving into a new house— really, everything that's coming up. And I know Ian didn't want to say it, but she's probably most afraid of me taking her dad away from her."

Having been a kid with a mother who drifted in and out of her life, I could relate to Peyton's need to stake a claim on the one parent she had left. "She's been through a lot with the loss of her mom."

"Which makes it all the more important that she knows that I'm not gonna be a wicked stepmother."

Rox arrived with Donna's wine. "Have you told her the plan yet?"

"I'm getting to it," Donna said, lifting her glass.

"Ooh, I'm just in time then." Rox gave me a nudge as she took the seat next to me. "I get to be part of this, too."

"Part of what exactly?" I hoped it wasn't some plan that got hatched because of something Donna had heard at Harmony House.

"Don't sound like such a worry wart," she said. "Your part's small, but since Peyton's so crazy about your dog, I'd really like him to be there."

"So all I'm expected to do is hold a leash? This isn't a speaking part?"

She grinned, probably because it sounded like I was

channeling my mother. "Think of it as a supporting role."

I looked across the table at Donna. "As long as Fozzie doesn't have to go to the clinic again, I'm in. Just tell me where and when."

"The Broward Park picnic area at noon."

I wasn't sure what I was getting myself into, but Fozzie was always up for a trip to the park. "Okay. It's a date."

Donna clapped. "Awesome! Here's the plan..."

"That was weird," Steve said two hours later, when he walked me to where I parked behind the bowling alley.

Loose gravel skittered around my espadrilles when I turned to look at him. "It wasn't weird. It was nice to see Donna looking so happy." And take a mental vacation from spinning my wheels on the Trevor Constantine murder.

"She smiled too much. Ian too. Something's up with them."

Hooking my arm around his, I pulled Steve toward the Subaru parked three spots down from his pickup. "You are such a cop. Always so suspicious."

"I just know what I saw."

"Okay."

"Okay, what?"

"Okay, I won't deny that you may have picked up on a little something they have planned," I said, unlocking my car door.

"Like what?"

"I've been sworn to secrecy."

"Not that I care, but are they eloping? 'Cause if they are, we don't have to get them a wedding present, right?"

I tossed my tote onto the passenger's seat. "You don't get out of going shopping with me that easily."

"And here I was hoping that we could use that valuable time doing something else," he said, wrapping his arms around me.

"What'd you have in mind?"

"A little of this, a little of that."

I linked my hands around his neck and delighted in his warmth as I held him tight. "Maybe I want more than a little of this."

"I think I can oblige," he said, lowering his lips to mine for a tender but all too brief kiss.

"More, please."

Steve planted another kiss on me. "So?"

"What?"

"Assuming the wedding's still on, what's up with them?"

I pushed away from him. "If you're using your wiles on me to get me to talk like in one of my mom's old spy movies, you should know that the script typically calls for at least five kisses."

"I'm not really the follow-the-script kind of guy."

"So I've noticed." I also noticed the bulge in his jeans.

"And I don't think you're the kind of girl to spill her guts after just five kisses."

"Yeah, probably not."

Steve undid the top two buttons of my blouse and ran his warm palm over my breast. "I like the feel of this."

He wasn't the only one.

"What's this fabric?"

"Silk."

"Very nice," he said, kissing his way down to the scalloped lace trim of my bra. "You smell good, too. Are you wearing some new perfume?"

"Nope."

"New soap?"

"No, nothing's different except..." *NO!* "I don't smell like disinfectant, do I?"

Steve's eyes were like pools of molten chocolate as he brushed back the wisps of hair the wind kept whipping into my face. "Why? Did you feel compelled to do some deep cleaning before you came over?"

"Not exactly." And I didn't want to ruin the mood by talking about work. "Forget I said anything and proceed with the wiles. You're doing great. I might even be ready to talk soon."

"Good to know."

Pinning me against my car with his body weight, he kissed me so long and deep my knees felt like melting butter.

"Well?" Steve asked, nuzzling my neck. "What do you think? Are my wiles working?"

"They're quite nice. Really first rate, but I'm still sworn to secrecy."

"Bummer." Straightening, he buttoned me back up. "I guess we're done here then."

"No, no, we're not done." I wrapped my arms around him.

"Oh? Something you'd like to say after all?"

"More like something I'd like you to do."

His gaze heated with carnal intent. "To you?"

That too. "*With* me, tomorrow at the park around twelve-thirty. If everything goes well, you'll see why Donna was smiling."

"That's it? That's all you're gonna tell me?"

"That's all I can say for now."

"Fine," he said, shaking his head.

"Then you'll come?"

"If you want me there, I'll be there."

"Good. I'll make a picnic lunch for us."

"Okay. Then I'll be sure to arrive hungry. Maybe we could even do something tonight to work up an appetite."

I pulled him close for a kiss. "I'm pretty sure we can think of something."

Chapter Thirty-One

With the sun beating down on me and Fozzie during our four-block walk to the park under a cloudless sky, the second to the last Saturday of May felt like it should be the first official day of summer.

Once we passed a boxy condominium complex of steel and glass, the Douglas firs lining the park loomed large to greet us while the six-acre green space behind them teemed with life.

Kids playing on a jungle gym, fathers and sons playing catch, moms pushing kids on swings, dogs being chased by toddlers, laughter, barking, a baby crying, phones ringing, birds chirping, music, seniors walking arm in arm on the gravel footpath, burgers grilling, rhododendrons with vibrant purple blooms, a gentle breeze rising from the glistening bay ruffling my hair.

Life in sunny Port Merritt was on glorious display. And as we crossed the street to the park entrance, Fozzie pulled on his leash as if he couldn't wait to be part of it.

"Hold up there, pup," I told him, letting him water the base of a scrubby pine tree while I waited for Donna to give me my cue.

Then, after receiving a text that she was ready for us, Fozzie and I hit the trail to the picnic area to look for Ian and Peyton.

We had just cleared the row of rocks marking the trailhead when a pretty brown-haired girl in denim shorts spotted us from her bench seat and started running.

"Fozzie!" Peyton squealed with her thin arms outstretched.

With an insulated beach tote swinging from my other hand, it was all I could do to keep my furball from jumping into those arms. "Hey, look who's here. Hi, Peyton!"

"I was hoping we'd see you today," she said while hugging Fozzie around the neck. "My dad said that you'd be coming. You know, because it's bark in the park day."

I was pretty sure that Ian had made that up. But fortunately, there were plenty of dogs here to mark this non-occasion. "We never want to miss bark in the park. It's one of Fozzie's favorite days."

"Mine too!" Peyton kissed the top of his head. "Especially now that you're here."

Sniffing her as if this little human should provide him a treat along with all this loving, Fozzie licked her chin with his black tongue.

Giggling, Peyton looked up at me. "Is he hungry? We have leftover hot dogs from lunch."

"He loves weenies, but only if you have enough."

"I'll find out." Peyton took off running toward a picnic table in the shade of a leafy maple tree.

"Well, hello there," I called out to Ian who had been

sitting alone with a bag of chips in front of him. "Fancy meeting you here."

"Yeah, small world." He gave me a thumbs-up when Peyton wasn't looking.

"Can Fozzie have a weenie?" she asked her dad.

Leaning over to open the insulated cooler on the grass, he broke off a bite-sized morsel and dropped it in Peyton's palm. "Because they're so salty, that's as much as he should have."

Really? I would have given him the entire wiener. *Oops.*

"Where's Donna?" I posed the question only because I was curious about what excuse she had given to make herself scarce.

"She had to get something from the car," Peyton said, enthralled by the dog licking her hand clean.

I set my tote down at the other end of the table. "Mind if we join you while we wait for her to come back?"

Ian looked past me and pointed. "She shouldn't be much longer."

I turned to see Donna approaching the picnic area with something wriggly in her arms while Rox followed with Alex in his stroller. "That's good." I waved, hoping that everything that was about to unfold would keep Ian and Peyton looking as happy as they did in that moment.

"May I take Fozzie for a walk to the dog park?" she asked me. "I promise we won't be gone long."

With Donna seconds away this was not the time for Peyton to run off with my dog.

Fortunately, I didn't have to worry about my next line because Ian took control of the situation. "Ms. Digby and Fozzie just got here. Let's give them a chance to get settled. Besides, I think I see Donna coming with dessert."

Peyton dropped onto the bench seat next to her dad. "I'm not hungry."

Ian ran his hand over her long ponytail. "Why don't you see what it is first."

"I don't need to see it." Her shoulders slumped. "I won't want it."

"Are you sure?" he said, pointing at the wiggly ball of fluff Donna was carrying.

Peyton straightened, her eyes wide with wonder when Donna handed her the golden retriever puppy. "What's going on?"

"This little guy needs a home." Donna smiled as she dropped to her knees in front of Peyton. "He's kind of like me. He's been wanting to be part of a family for the longest time, and I thought... If it's okay with you, we could all be a family together."

After a couple of beats of silence that felt like forever, Peyton nodded. Relief washed over Donna's face, and Rox and I exchanged smiles.

I also released a breath I hadn't realized I'd been holding.

Holding the little furball tight, Peyton turned to her dad with tears pooling in her eyes. "I didn't think we could have a dog."

"That's because your grandmother is allergic, but we'll be living at our new house soon," Ian said. "So there's no reason why we can't adopt this puppy. Assuming, of course, that you help take care of him."

"I will, I promise." Peyton giggled when the puppy nuzzled her while wagging his tail. "I think he likes me."

"Of course he does," Donna said, wiping away Peyton's tears with the pad of her thumb. "He's going to be your buddy for a very long time."

Peyton smiled down at the fluffy puppy in her lap. "Will you be my buddy? Hey, we could even name him Buddy."

Donna nodded. "That's an excellent name."

"I think so too," Ian said, chucking the pup under the chin. "Welcome to the family, Buddy."

Peyton looked to her dad. "Where's Buddy gonna live until we move?"

"With me at my apartment," Donna said. "The house closes at the end of the month, so he and I will move in then. And of course, we'll see you every day to go for walks, and then you'll need to come over and decorate your bedroom and help me figure out where things should go. So there will be lots and lots of opportunities for you two to spend time together."

With you to start building that family bond. Good one, Donna.

Ian gently tugged on his daughter's ponytail. "How's that sound, sweetie?"

"Good." Peyton fixed her gaze on Buddy. "But we might need to have some sleepovers too. You know, so Buddy doesn't get lonely."

"Excellent idea! Maybe starting tonight if it's okay

with your dad." Donna got to her feet and took his hand. "Who will need to get Buddy's carrier out of Roxie's car and upstairs to my apartment. She's parked right behind us."

"No problem. I can do that right now." Rising from the bench seat, Ian extended his palm to Rox. "Keys, please."

She handed him a key ring with a fob, and to Peyton who was standing behind him with a squirming puppy, Rox offered the thin red leash she pulled from a compartment of Alex's stroller. "Clip this onto Buddy's collar and I bet he'll be happy to follow your lead."

"Look, Daddy!" Peyton called out, scampering after him with the bounding little retriever. "Look how he can run already."

"Running isn't a problem for that pup." Rox leaned over to soothe Alex when he started crying. "I practically had to corral him to get him into that carrier."

Tugging at his leash to follow Peyton, Fozzie came back to my side when I offered him one of the biscuits I had tucked in a pocket of my tote. While he crunched, Donna walked toward me with a bright smile.

"Happy?" I asked, although I didn't need to. The spring in her step spoke volumes.

"Very. Thanks for your help." She gave me a squeezy hug and then turned to Rox, who was bouncing a fussy baby in her arms. "Thank you, both. We couldn't have pulled this off without you."

"You know we were happy to help," Rox said. "It was fun to have a puppy in the house, but I think we'll wait a couple of years to get a dog." She grinned. "Or have another baby. All I know is that I don't want to deal with any more pee and poop than absolutely necessary right now."

Donna caressed Alex's cheek. "When you put it that way, me neither. But by the time Ian and I make one of these, Buddy should be housebroken."

All this baby talk was making my biological clock clang like an alarm going off in my head. "Trust me as a dog owner, you'll still be dealing with pee and poop," I said to change the subject. "A never-ending supply."

Fozzie woofed as if to back up my statement, but then I realized his tail was wagging at the sight of one of his favorite humans on the gravel footpath.

Mine, too. I waved at Steve while Fozzie tugged at his leash to greet him.

"Am I too early?" Steve asked, looking from me to Donna while he gave Fozzie a pat on his back. "I wouldn't want to interrupt some secret handshake thing that you girls have got going."

I gave him a quick hug. "You're right on time."

"Yeah, we're all out of secret handshakes, so boys are allowed now," Rox added with a smirk.

Donna smiled at him. "I just needed to borrow Char for a few minutes so that I could smooth something over. It was sort of a girl thing."

Steve pointed at the girl cradling the puppy in her arms, followed by her father. "It looks to me that it wasn't just girls at this shindig. Who's this little guy?"

"This is Buddy. We just got him," Peyton proudly announced. "He's not very good at walking with a leash yet. He kept getting tangled up in it."

Donna put her arm around Peyton's shoulder. "That's something that you two will need to practice, and there will be plenty of room to do that in that big backyard we're gonna have."

Ian greeted Steve and then picked up the cooler he'd left by the picnic table. "In the meantime, Peyton, you can practice in Grandma's yard and then pack for tonight's sleepover. How's that sound?"

"Great! Let's go," she said, taking off for the car with Buddy.

"That sounded like a yes vote," Donna chuckled, giving me another hug. "Thanks again, and thank you, Fozzie. You helped make a girl very happy."

Actually two, but who was counting?

After a round of good-byes, Steve and I watched as Rox, Donna, and Donna's soon-to-be-family left the park.

At least I was watching them. I glanced over to see Steve looking at me. "What?"

"You're smiling, kind of like Donna was last night."

"I can't help it. I'm a sucker for happy endings."

"So I take it the secret plan worked."

"Seemed to."

"And it involved a puppy."

"Yep," I said, securing Fozzie's leash to a leg of the picnic table.

"Anything else you'd like to volunteer about what went down here, or do you want me to use more of my wiles on you to make you talk?"

"Ooh, more wiles, please." I wrapped my arms around his waist. "Starting with a kiss hello."

"Hello," he said, planting a chaste peck on my lips.

"You can do better than that."

And he did.

Chapter Thirty-Two

My Monday wasn't off to an auspicious start.

I spilled my mocha latte in the car on my way to work.

The copying project Patsy had given me had consumed most of the morning because the fricking copier overheated three times.

But worst of all, after talking Steve into meeting me at noon at the Shabby Apple antique store, he was a no-show.

"Where are you?" I asked him, looking down Main Street with my cell phone pressed to my ear and seeing only Carmen jaywalking as she left Clark's Pharmacy.

"I was about to call you. The captain asked me to stand in for him at a lunch meeting with the town council, so I'm gonna have to bail on our shopping date."

"And I don't suppose you mentioned to him that you already had lunch plans."

"Sorry, Chow Mein."

"You don't sound very sorry," I said over the rumble of the logging truck passing by. "I swear, you'll do anything to get out of going shopping with me."

"Not true. Not entirely, anyway. Besides, you know the guy better than I do. Just pick something out. I'm sure it'll be fine."

"Barry's birthday present is supposed to be from the two of us. You know, something nice that we *both* put some thought into."

"I trust that you'll put enough thought into it for the two of us."

"Very helpful," I said, watching a blue pickup with the Havens Berry Farm logo on the door pull into a parking spot thirty feet away from me.

"Meeting's about to start. Gotta go."

Steve disconnected, leaving me alone on the sidewalk with Carmen rushing toward me with her hand out-stretched as if she were hailing a taxi.

I thought about ducking into the Shabby Apple to avoid the next ten minutes of gossip that would surely follow, but then noticed the woman with the pink hair climbing out of the pickup with Rory Havens, and I froze.

"Oh, Charmaine," Carmen said between labored breaths. "How fortuitous to run into you. I wanted to ask you about that psychic you and Donna went to."

Harmony Peel was the last person I wanted to chat about, especially with her next-door neighbor within earshot.

"You must have me confused with someone else." I smiled, giving a little wave to Amity and Mr. Havens as they entered the law office two doors down from the Shabby Apple.

"I don't think so. Miriam said—"

"Miriam's source might not be the most reliable." I should have felt worse lying to Carmen, but then I noticed that she wasn't paying attention to me. She was focused on that door closing behind Mr. Havens.

"Hunh," she grunted. "There's something I never thought I'd see."

I wasn't sure what we had just witnessed. "What?"

"Rory Havens spending any time with his former daughter-in-law. Gaylene always made it sound like he could barely tolerate the girl."

"They were family once. Maybe there's still some sort of bond."

"Hmmm, maybe. Of course, her husband just died, so I can understand her turning to Rory to get the name of an attorney to help her settle the estate."

That seemed likely to me, too. But after seeing the two of them together in that video, today's sighting felt a lot more significant.

"What I don't get is why Rory would want to be with her," Carmen said, scratching under the band of her floppy white hat. "It's the middle of a work day for him, so this is very strange."

"I'm sure there's a logical reason." I just wished I knew what it was.

"I'm gonna find out what Lucille knows about it."

Which probably wouldn't be much, but that was what I'd be doing if I didn't have a birthday present to buy.

After we said our good-byes and Carmen disappeared inside Duke's, I walked to the law office I had delivered some witness statements to earlier in the year.

Affixed to a shingle next to the door were three en-graved name plates for the law office of Pettybone, Durante, and Wilson. But just the names, nothing that indicated their specialties, which didn't help explain why Mr. Havens had brought Amity here. All I knew was that I needed to head back to the Shabby Apple before anyone who might be waiting in the lobby spotted me.

Unfortunately, that was when I spotted Lucille race-walking toward me with a white bakery bag like she was trying out for some Olympic delivery event.

"Are they still in there?" Lucille called out.

I shushed her. "What are you doing?"

She waved me off as she blew by me. "What does it look like I'm doing? I'm makin' a delivery."

"You're not really going in there."

"Watch me," Lucille said, reaching for the law office door.

Wanting no part of whatever happened next, I ducked into the Shabby Apple, where the musty odor of the vin-tage clutter lining the shelves assailed my nostrils.

Mrs. Dewsbury, the silver-haired owner, looked up from the Tiffany lamp she was dusting. "May I help you find something, Charmaine?"

"I wish you could." In so many ways.

Her smile slipped. "Is something wrong?"

Other than an unsolved murder making some of us a little crazier than usual?

"No, everything's fine," I said, looking back over my shoulder to see Lucille heading back to Duke's. "But I need to get back to work and just wanted to check to see how late you were open."

"Until six. Same as it's been for the last thirty years."

In other words, having worked up the street from her for quite a few of those years, I should have asked a smarter question. Oh well.

"Perfect. I'll be back later. Thanks, Mrs. Dewsbury!"

I dashed out the door and ran to catch up with Lucille outside of Duke's. "Well? What'd you find out?"

"Not a lot. Candace, the receptionist, is pretty tight-lipped when it comes to the clientele, but she's also a big fan of Alice's German chocolate cake, so I knew she'd be good for a few crumbs of reciprocation."

"And?"

Lucille looked up and down the sidewalk, and tsked when she spotted Miriam rounding the corner. "Not out here."

She held the door open for me, Duke eyeballing us as the silver bell announced our arrival.

"Nice of you to rejoin us," he groused to Lucille as we zipped into the kitchen to avoid Carmen's prying eyes. "I'm not paying you to run off, you know."

Lucille squeaked past his grill without slowing. "I took a little break, so sue me."

He grimaced at me as I went by. "She seems to take a lot more breaks when you're around. Explain that to me."

"Coincidence?" I quipped, trying to keep the mood light so that he wouldn't throw me out of his kitchen. "I'm just here for a tuna sandwich to go."

Duke grunted. "Sure you are."

"Uh-oh," Alice said, looking up with her rolling pin in hand as Lucille and I approached. "What's this about you running off? Did something happen?"

Taking the stool next to Alice, Lucille leaned on her elbows. "Carmen saw Rory Havens take his former daughter-in-law in to see Ken Durante."

Alice frowned. "A lawyer."

Lucille nodded. "Not just any lawyer. *His* lawyer, according to Candace, and the appointment was for the two of 'em."

"Okay, so despite all the water under the bridge with the way she left his son high and dry, Rory's helping her settle the estate," Alice said, glancing across the table at me. "Or am I wrong about that, because you have a funny look on your face."

Probably because I was trying to understand why Rory Havens would do such a thing for Amity. The only answer I could think of that made sense was to take some control over the situation. And that would only be if he had some interest to protect. "That's my confused face, because I don't know any more than you do."

"That's all Candace would tell you?" I asked Lucille.

She nodded. "That's all she wrote."

Which wasn't much, but it sure made me wonder what Rory Havens was up to.

Chapter Thirty-Three

After making a quick trip back to Mrs. Dewsbury's shop before it closed, where I purchased a hand-painted Tudor kings and queens chess set that I thought Barry would enjoy—plus, it was the only classy thing in the stop that Marietta wouldn't thumb her nose at—I headed home to bake the birthday cake she had requested.

"Death by chocolate" was how Barry had fondly referred to the cake that I baked last August for my mother's birthday. Thick chocolate cream cheese icing and ganache sandwiched between four delectable layers of dark chocolate.

Definitely a dessert to die for, but every step of the way, from the stop I made at the Red Apple Market to my last drizzle of ganache, I couldn't stop thinking about Amity.

Was she being pressured to do something by her former in-laws?

If she was as innocent of her husband's murder as Harmony and Clio, and even Killian said she was, could she be vulnerable to blackmail if Rory Havens thought he had something on her?

Or worse, if whatever he was up to had left Trevor dead.

The next evening, after a boring day of busywork, I fed Fozzie, packed up Barry's cake, and then rushed to Duke's to help Alice with the salads she was bringing to round out the barbecue dinner my mother had planned.

"How's it going?" I called out when the kitchen screen door banged shut behind me. "Can I do anything to help?"

Alice pulled out a plastic-covered aluminum bowl of pasta salad from the refrigerator and set it next to an identical bowl of potato salad. "Put these in your car, but first tell me what Rory Havens is up to."

I wished I knew.

"Because I've been thinking about that visit to his lawyer all day." She plopped down on a stool. "Something's fishy about it."

"Not necessarily," I said, taking the stool next to her. "There could be a reasonable explanation for it."

Skepticism tugged at her thin lips. "Yeah? Well, I know Gaylene Havens pretty darn well, and the stuff she's told me about that girl Killian married... Let's just say that there's no love lost between them."

"Then why would Mr. Havens take Amity to see his attorney?"

"That's what I can't figure."

"You girls make everything so dang complicated." Duke walked over after hanging up his apron. "The reason's obvious."

Not to me it wasn't. "Which is?"

"Think about it," he said. "When do you go to a law-yer?"

To get a divorce.

Probably not the answer he was looking for, but that was the most common reason in my family. "When you need to write a will, or in Amity's case, because she needs some legal advice regarding the business she plans on selling."

"Plus, the estate will have to go through probate," Alice added.

He clapped as if we had passed his pop quiz with flying colors. "Yep, that's where Ken comes in."

And that's where Duke lost me. "Yes, but why would Amity want Rory Havens to sit in on something that shouldn't concern him?" Because I couldn't imagine sitting down with my ex-husband's father over a year after my divorce, especially if it involved my finances.

"She has something he wants." Duke nodded as if I should be able to put two and two together.

"You're not talking about the business," Alice shot back.

"Woman, you know as well as I do, Havens has been after that land behind the barn forever."

This was the first time I was hearing about this. "So Mr. Havens isn't doing this to help Amity. He's grabbing hold of an opportunity to help himself."

When his former daughter-in-law was at her most vulnerable. "I sure hope that lawyer didn't talk her into anything."

Duke shrugged a meaty shoulder. "Hey, if she's not

smart enough to get her own lawyer, that's her problem."

Could Gaylene and Rory Havens really be that cold-blooded?

Since Trevor Constantine ended up dead in the first act of this apparent land grab, I hated to believe that the answer to that question was yes.

Duke rubbed his hands together as if that should be the last word on this subject. "Are we ready to go? We're supposed to be there in an hour and some of us still need to get cleaned up."

"I'll take the salads and meet you there." After a brief detour that I hoped wouldn't take more than an hour.

Putting the pedal to the metal of my Subaru, I made it to Amity's house twenty-five minutes later.

Unlike my last visit, Max greeted me with a wagging tail when I crawled out of my car. "Hi, Max. I'm glad to see that we're friends now."

"He's a pretty good judge of people," Amity called out, holding a wineglass as she looked down at me from her porch. "Plus, he just ate and had a walk, so he's in a pretty mellow mood."

I flashed her a friendly smile. "That always works for me."

Wearing cutoffs with a sleeveless gauzy blouse that coordinated nicely with the blues and greens of her feather tattoo, Amity looked pretty mellow herself. "What brings you here?"

"I was in the neighborhood." In a very roundabout way.

She raised her glass. "Want something to drink?"

"Sure." It gave us an excuse to go inside and talk. Exactly what I needed. "Just half a glass, though. I can't stay long."

I followed her into the kitchen, where Amity grabbed a long-stemmed wineglass from a mostly empty shelf and poured from an open bottle of champagne.

Not my first choice of beverages, but I could choke down some cheap bubbly if it bought me a few minutes of time with her.

The cardboard boxes consuming most of her counter space told me where the former occupants of her cupboards had gone. "Looks like you won't be staying much longer either."

"I found an apartment in Port Townsend that'll be available at the end of the month. So I'll soon be outta here." Amity handed me the wineglass and clinked it with her own. "Which can't happen soon enough."

"Seeing you visit that attorney yesterday, it seems like a lot of things are happening right now."

"They need to."

"That's actually why I'm here."

She narrowed her eyes. "Because you saw me at a lawyer's office yesterday?"

"With Rory Havens."

"Yeah, and...?"

"I'm concerned that he might not be the best advocate to look after your interests."

Leaning against the counter, a smile crept across Amity's lips as she sipped her champagne. "I'm not sure why you should be concerned at all, but whatever."

"It's just that I work with a bunch of attorneys and if you need a recommendation, I'm sure I could get you a couple of names—"

"I got a lawyer already," she said, giving her two-tone pigtails a jiggle "Besides, everything's a done deal, or at least soon will be."

That gave me the sinking feeling that we were having this conversation a day too late. "What's a done deal?"

"The sale."

"Of what?"

A glow of satisfaction infused her cheeks. "The business."

That sounded like a lot more than the acre of weeds that my mother was mowing last weekend. "Your husband's farm supply business?"

"The business, the buildings, the property." Amity raised her glass in celebration. "I'm selling everything but Trev's truck out there."

Holy cannoli! "Who to?"

Chapter Thirty-Four

"What do you mean, she sold to Rory Havens?" Alice demanded, hot on my heels as I carried the bowl of pasta salad into my mother's kitchen.

"Just what I said. Amity sold the business and all the property to him."

"What'd Rory do? Make her an offer she couldn't refuse?"

That's what I wondered. "All I know is that she seemed perfectly content with it."

"She who?" Gram asked, entering the kitchen with an almost-empty wineglass.

Alice glanced over her shoulder at her sister. "Amity Constantine. Get over here. You're gonna want to hear this."

"Ooh, gossip." Gram grinned. "I usually miss out on all of Lucille's latest news. What've you got?"

"This news is courtesy of your granddaughter," Alice said as she shuffled the contents of Marietta's refrigerator to make room for the pasta salad.

Gram turned to me. "Well? Let's have it."

"I don't have any details, but Amity told me that she's

selling Constantine Farm Supply to Rory Havens."

Gram sucked in a breath. "Really. But Dorothy had made it sound like that girl wanted to hold out for top dollar from an outsider."

"Technically, I guess Rory is an outsider," Alice said. "But if he just wanted to expand into that property, why would he pay top dollar for the equipment inventory that would go with it?"

"Oh, are y'all talking about Rory buying that place that sold me the riding mower?" Marietta said, sashaying in on a wave of musky jasmine to give me a peck on the cheek. "And hello, sugar, it's about time you got here. We're all starving."

I was sixteen minutes late. Not that any of her guests cared since they had all been in the backyard, taking turns in the driver's seat of Barry's birthday present.

"Where's the cake?" My mother scanned her kitchen, panic flashing in her eyes. "Please don't tell me you forgot about the cake!"

I took a silent three-count to squelch the heavy sigh bubbling to my lips. "The cake's fine. It's chilling in my air-conditioned car at the moment." And was probably more capable of keeping its cool than I was.

"Thank goodness! Don't scare your mama that way. But why don't we bring it in. It's time for the festivities to begin now that we're all here."

Not so fast. "What do you know about Rory Havens buying the farm supply?"

"A little birdie shared the big news with me when the lawnmower was delivered this afternoon," my mother said in the annoying singsong voice she used to amuse herself.

I couldn't stand that voice growing up, and I hated it even more now. "The name of the birdie?"

"I can't remember his name, Charmaine." She flicked a bangled wrist in my direction. "You know, the gentleman who sold me the lawnmower."

"That would be Neil." Gram pointed at her daughter. "Really, Mary Jo, you'd think you'd remember the name of the man you almost maimed."

It was time to pull on the reins of this conversation before it galloped away from me. "Mom, what exactly did Neil tell you?"

She heaved a petulant sigh. "I don't remember *exactly*. It was something about us both having something to celebrate today. I thought at first that he was referring to a graduation or something, but then he told me it was a family celebration. That they'd be breaking out the champagne because Rory bought the business."

"But if he did that to turn all that property into farmland," I looked at Gram, "how is this something for the Constantines to celebrate? I thought that was their worst nightmare. That Amity would sell and then they'd all be out of a job."

"Sounds like some people worry too much to me." Steve crossed the kitchen to give me a kiss. "Overthink stuff too much, too."

I didn't have to guess who he was referring to. "You obviously know something about this, so how about sharing with the rest of the class."

"Yeah." Alice planted her hands on her hips. "If you know something, spill it."

"There's not a lot to spill," Steve said, leaning against the counter. "I ran into Dorothy Constantine when I was out for a coffee and heard her telling Miriam that their business was saved. Sounded to me like Rory met with Neil to ask him to stay on and run the operation."

"Not that I told you so, but…" Duke's booming voice filled the kitchen as he sidled up next to his wife. "Rory just wants the land in the back to expand the farm. Everything else is just an investment."

Alice glared at him. "You knew about this?"

"Just that it's been in the works for a few days," Duke said. "Rory mentioned that he'd made an offer when he made Monday's delivery."

Maybe that explained what he was doing over at Amity's house.

Alice swatted Duke's arm. "And you didn't tell me? What's wrong with you?"

He shrugged. "He asked me to keep it on the down low."

Alice swatted him again. "But I'm your wife. You're supposed to keep me in the loop!"

"Yeah, right. Then you'd tell Lucille, and Lucille would tell Miriam, and then someone would need to get their hair done and blab over there. I wasn't born yesterday. I know how news travels in these parts."

"Then that's that," Marietta announced to the crowd assembled in her kitchen. "It's good news all around, so let's start grilling while the barbecue's hot."

My grandmother shook her head. "Who can think about food right now? What about the murder?"

My question exactly.

"Yeah." Alice frowned at Steve. "Just because Rory has become the Constantines' hero for buying the business doesn't mean that he should come off smelling like a rose. He could have set all this in motion by bumping off Trevor."

With a quirk of amusement at his lips, Steve folded his arms across his chest. "And why would he want to do that?"

"Maybe Trevor wouldn't sell to him," Gram answered for her sister. "Emotions were running too high because of Killian hanging around his wife." She glanced in my direction. "That's certainly the impression I got when we were chatting with Leah that day."

Steve leveled his gaze on me. "Chatting or pumping anyone related to Trevor for information?"

"We were simply making conversation while my mom was shopping. I hadn't seen Leah in such a long time." Something that was conveniently true. "It would've been rude not to."

"Right," he muttered.

"Back to the murder, though." Gram glanced at me. "I really don't think we should eliminate Rory Havens as a suspect. After all, we just found out how much he had to gain after Trevor's death. Shouldn't that be considered as motive?"

Steve breathed in and out as if he wanted to choose his words carefully. Probably so that he wouldn't put any future pot roast dinners into jeopardy. "Eleanor, I have it on good authority that several customers gave Rory an alibi that morning. You being one of them."

"He did seem to be wandering in and out of his greenhouses, doing his watering while we were there," Gram said, looking at me for backup.

"Not the entire time," I added. "Just most of the time."

Steve aimed a fake smile at me. "Did he have any blood on him at any time?"

"Not that I noticed." On anyone I saw there that day.

"Did his behavior change at any time you were around him?" Steve didn't wait for me to answer. "Was he sweating? Did he give off any signals that he was nervous?"

"No." But I was getting increasingly nervous with all the eyes in this kitchen staring at me.

"Then I think he smells as close to a rose as a guy can probably get." Steve came up behind me and lowered his voice. "So accept that you and your granny are barking up the wrong tree on this one."

Fine.

"Are we done with all that dreadful murder business now?" my mother asked, giving me the stink eye as if I had been the one to bring the bloody knife to her doorstep. "Because some of us would like to eat sometime tonight."

"Yes," I grumbled. "I'll get the cake."

"I'll help you," Steve said, following me to the front door. "Your grandmother couldn't have really believed that Rory Havens would kill a guy to take over his business."

"It was more of a working theory that some people were considering."

"Yeah, some people." He turned off my ignition and handed me my keys. "Some of those same people need to let this go."

So I'd heard.

Chapter Thirty-Five

"Why are we stopped in the middle of the street?" Marietta asked, fluffing her cropped hair in the mirrored visor for the third time since I picked her up bright and way too early on this Saturday morning. "We're here. Let's park the car and go in."

"We're a little early." Amity had wanted us to arrive at Le Calme an hour before they opened the doors at nine. "It's not eight o'clock yet." Which was extremely early for Marietta to be anywhere in full hair and makeup other than a movie set. "Don't you think—"

"What I think is that I've done a lot more of these appearances than you." Offering her reflection a toothy smile, she checked for lipstick smudges. "They always want the talent to arrive early."

I was tempted to remind the "talent" sitting next to me that we were going to a day spa and not a red carpet event. "Uh-huh."

"Oh," she bleated as if she were deflating while I parked in front of the used bookstore next door. "I thought they'd do more than that with my headshot."

Shutting off the ignition, I strained to see what she

was looking at. "Where?"

"Exactly the problem." She pointed at the sandwich board on the sidewalk. "You can't read my name or see that little picture of me from a distance."

"Well, it's not like it's a movie theater with a marquee," I said, grabbing my tote.

Stepping out of the car, she aimed a month's worth of side eye at me. "I'm well aware, Charmaine. I'm just saying that I was led to expect that they were going to do something a little splashier in the way of advertising. The flyers Amity and her friends posted around town turned out okay, but..."

"Sorry." With all the focus on the grand opening, Brooke and Joel probably didn't have the time or money to do anything beyond running an ad in the local paper.

"No matter. There's nothing to be done about it now." Pulling her shoulders back, Marietta lifted her chin as if she were getting into character. "Let it go. Let it go. Let it go."

Jeez, not you too.

"There, all better." She turned to use the reflection of the bookstore window to smooth the persimmon wraparound dress clinging to her curves and then licked her glossy lips. "What do you think, sugar? Will I do?"

Was she kidding? Marietta Moreau may have slipped off the D-list after hitting the big five-oh, but she could still play the part of local celebrity with dazzling aplomb. "Mom, you always do extremely nicely."

She beamed as she strutted toward the spa's entrance in her four-inch stiletto slingbacks. "Right answer."

"Hello, hello," Marietta called out as she knocked on the locked door.

When there was no answer, she looked back at me. "Are we really that early?"

Wasn't that what I just said? "A little. Knock again."

After a few seconds of shouting, Brooke came to the door with her hair up in curlers and a harried look in her eyes. "Sorry, we were in the middle of something, and I didn't realize it was that late."

"No, honey," Marietta said, falling back into her Georgia accent as if the *Peachtree Girls* cameras were rolling. "I told my daughtah I feared we were arrivin' a little too early."

Liar!

"I do hope we're not inconveniencin' y'all."

Brooke looked at my mother and her fake accent with the resting bitch face of a runway model. "No, not at all."

Another great big lie.

I had a feeling this was going to be a long, miserable day, and I hadn't even been guilted for the state of my ragged cuticles yet.

"Perhaps I could ask you to step into our waiting area for a couple of minutes while I get ready." Brooke squeezed out an insincere smile as she led us into a sterile-looking room with four ivory upholstered chairs, a gleaming marble floor, and pale sage walls.

"I promise to be quick," she added, her smile crumbling at the sound of the angry exchange taking place in a back room.

"Joel!" I heard a female voice shout.

276 | WENDY DELANEY

Glancing behind her, Brooke looked like a deer caught in headlights. "Um... sorry about that. Things are a little nuts today." She pointed at the glass decanter next to the white glossy reception desk. "Help yourself to some kiwi and lemon—infused water. We feature it as part of our detox—"

"No, we can't do this another time!" the mystery female yelled.

Brooke's head turned as if it were on a swivel. "I have to..."

"Do what you need to do, honey," Marietta said, flicking a bangled wrist, but Brooke had already run off down the hall. "Because all is clearly not well."

No kidding.

"Everything looks lovely, far exceeding my expectation considering how this place looked last year, but it doesn't sound as if Le Calme is ready to live up to its name." Marietta peeked around the corner when Brooke's voice added to the volume of the backroom argument. "In fact, it sounds quite the opposite."

"I'm sure it's none of our business," I said, pouring myself a cup of kiwi water. "It's probably going to be more than a couple of minutes, so why don't you sit down. Want some water?"

"Sure, I love kiwis. Obviously, someone else here does, too. Kiwis in their water, kiwis in some of their treatments."

She took a chair while I poured and started reading aloud from the list of spa treatments posted on the sign mounted above my head. "That kiwi-cucumber facial sounds delightful."

What didn't sound delightful was the screaming woman in the other room.

"Joel, explain this to me," someone yelled, but it didn't sound like Brooke. It sounded more like Amity.

"Mom, wait here a minute. I'm going to see if they need some help."

I handed my mother a paper cup and then followed my ears past a manicure station and two treatment rooms to the end of a dimly lit hall, where a mirrored wall fountain trickled as if it didn't have a care in the world. But the same couldn't be said for the kitchen behind it, because standing in front of Joel was Brooke, hurling obscenities at Amity.

"Back off, Brooke," Amity shouted, pushing her toward a refrigerator with a roller derby-type jab.

Brooke's eyes went to me as I stood at the door as if she were shooting darts. "I asked you to wait in the reception area."

While some sort of fight had broken out back here? Not a chance. "I heard the commotion and thought I should see if you were okay."

"Oh, don't worry about her," Amity said with her gaze fixed on Joel. "She's been doing just fine."

Brooke lapsed back into her bitch face. "I've told you, it's not at all what you think. Tell her, Joel."

"Let's go upstairs to my office," he said, his face shiny with sweat as he tried to steer Amity by the elbow. "I'll make us some coffee."

"I don't want any coffee." Shaking him off, she held

up a sheet of paper that looked like a legal document. "What I want is answers."

"Get her out of here first," Joel barked, looking like a muscled-up bouncer who would relish the opportunity to throw me out on my ear.

"Nobody moves until you tell me what this is about," Amity announced.

I felt like that was my cue to sit down and play the neutral observer, so I took a seat at the dinette table in the corner.

"Start talking," she demanded.

Joel shook his head. "Not with her here."

"She's staying," Amity stated with an icy resolve. "She's my advocate."

I almost choked on the last swallow of my water.

She turned to me. "That's the term you used the other night, right?"

Yes, but it wasn't like I could offer her anything beyond moral support. "That's the one."

"So she's helping me with legal stuff like this." She aimed that paper at his nose. "And we're not leaving until we get an explanation."

"Listen, we're supposed to open in less than an hour," he said with his feet inching toward the door. "Let's talk tonight and celebrate the opening. I'll buy."

"You'll buy?!" Amity grinned but there wasn't a glimmer of anything worth celebrating in her eyes. "With what? Trevor's money?"

What?

"What's that supposed to mean?" Brooke asked Joel.

"What's she talking about?"

"The fifty thousand he owed Trevor!" Tears streamed down Amity's face. "Oh, Joel, what did you do?"

The color drained from his face, his gaze ping-ponging between Amity and Brooke. "Nothing. She's confused. Everything's fine."

No, it wasn't.

"I'm not confused." Amity fell into the chair next to me, her breathing ragged as she used her shirtsleeve to wipe her eyes. "I-I have the proof right here."

I grabbed a napkin from the holder in front of me and handed it to her.

While she blew her nose, I thought it was my duty as her advocate to take a look at the "proof" she had set down between us.

At first glance, her proof looked rather unimpressive, boilerplate, clearly a form created using a template. But once I read the words, *promissory note*, and saw the signatures at the bottom, my heart started thumping.

Joel Stillwell, the "maker" of the note, promised to pay Trevor Constantine fifty thousand dollars. It was a guaranteed debt, maker's responsibility to repay after a term of one year, blah, blah, blah. Signed and dated May first of last year.

Which meant that the note was due.

In fact, if Joel had yet to pay up, it was past due.

And considering that fifty thousand was such a tidy sum, I assumed that Trevor would have contacted his buddy Joel with a polite reminder that it was time to pay his debt.

And if Joel needed more time because of the work they were still doing on the spa, and he went over to Trevor's house to talk to his pal about it and whatever renegotiation he attempted didn't go well...

I shivered, hearing the echo of Harmony's words in my head. *"It's time."*

"This note is past due, Joel," I said, trying to act the part of an advocate while my skin crawled with goose-flesh.

He shook his head. "No, we had an arrangement."

I tapped the note. "That's not what this says."

"That's old, outdated." Joel slanted a nervous glance at Brooke, who was staring at him in stunned silence.

"You remember me from growing up around here, right?" He should have, because I sure remembered him. "You realize that I can tell that you're lying."

"You should shut up. You don't know what you're talking about." He turned to Brooke. "You need to get ready to open while I get things settled here."

Tears spilled over her spiky lashes. "You had to ask Trevor for money?"

Joel winced. "It was just a business arrangement."

"That was needed because of what happened with my mom?" Brooke asked, smearing her mascara as she wiped her eyes.

"No, baby. I told you that you didn't need to worry when she couldn't give us the money she promised."

Barbara had planned to give them another chunk of the funds she embezzled? Not having a fat balance in the bank would have been a problem for these two, especially when the bill arrived to pay for their fancy marble floors.

"Didn't I tell you that you should've asked more questions about where he was getting the financing after your mom backed out?" Amity snapped at Brooke. "Really, how'd you think you were paying for all this?"

It sounded as if Amity had put two and two together and it added up to her husband paying for all that marble—ultimately with his life.

"I thought we got another bank loan. We had money in our account, so I thought everything was going okay." Brooke reached for a napkin as the waterworks flowed. "We just needed to get through this remodel. My mom's trial too. Everything was going to be okay once we got back to normal."

Joel choked back a humorless chuckle as he leaned against the refrigerator.

Clearly, he hadn't been sharing how not okay everything had been going.

"It was at least fifty thousand that you had been counting on to help finance the remodel, right, Joel?" I said. "Barbara got busted in late April. It's some coincidence that you asked your pal for a loan a couple of days later."

Squeezing his eyes shut, Joel shook his head.

"What did you do? Give yourself a year to complete the remodel, re-open, and start raking in the dough so you could pay Trevor back?" I waited for him to give me some indication that I had made a good guess, but I heard nothing but the sound of Brooke's sniffling while Joel continued to shake his head.

His non-denial did enough to inform me that I was on the right track.

"And then sometime after January, someone decided that they wanted to transform this place into a destination spot. What did you call it, Brooke? A beauty and wellness oasis?"

She gave me a smeary-eyed blank stare.

"That has to cost some bucks. Probably a lot more than you borrowed. And with no money coming in yet and some hefty bills adding up..."

Brooke's stare sharpened as she turned it on her betrothed. "What exactly is she saying?"

Joel hung his head.

"She's saying that he killed my husband," Amity whispered as if that was all the volume she had the energy for.

"I'm going to make a call," I told her as I pushed out of my chair. "Can you stick around for a few minutes?" *A nice detective will want to talk to you.*

She nodded. "But I don't want to stay in here with *him*."

Completely understandable. "Why don't you come with me because I have to hang out here a little while, too."

Amity followed me to the reception area, where Marietta was standing expectantly.

"Is everything okay?" Her gaze softened as she took a tearful Amity into her arms. "Oh, dear, I can see that it's not."

"Sit with her for a minute. I have to call Steve."

My mother looked up at me as she eased into the seat next to Amity. "Make it quick. I have to pee."

Stifling a sigh, I picked up the paper cup next to her chair. "How many of these did you have?"

"Four but they're very small."

"Don't drink any more until I get back," I said on my way out the door. Because I had enough on my plate without having to deal with my mother's tiny bladder.

Five seconds later, Steve picked up on the first ring. Ten seconds after a brief outburst of swearing, he told me that he was on his way.

"Done with your call?" Marietta flashed me a brittle smile as I locked the door behind me.

I nodded.

"Where do you think the little girls' room is?"

"Last room on the right," Amity said.

When Marietta's heels clicked away on that shiny marble, I poured some water for Amity and me.

"It'll just be a few minutes for the police to get here," I said, sitting down next to her. "The sheriff is being notified too."

Amity nodded and took a sip of water.

I glanced toward the door and noticed that a couple of older ladies were outside, waiting for the grand opening that wouldn't be happening, at least not today.

They'd be disappointed, but no more than my mother, who'd had her heart set on getting some star treatment followed up by a free facial.

"It shouldn't be much longer," I said, hearing a siren in the distance, which probably meant that a patrol unit had been dispatched.

"Yeah."

She'd obviously heard the siren, too.

After several beats of silence between us, she asked, "How did you know so much about Brooke's mom?"

"I work for the county prosecutor and sat in for part of her trial."

"Yeah, you said you worked for attorneys."

"Out of curiosity, when did you find the promissory note?" I asked Amity.

"Last night. I was going through all the estate papers Trevor had in a safe at the house, and found it."

That was some find. "If you hadn't done that, his murder might have gone unsolved."

She sighed. "I wanted answers. I still don't understand what happened. Why Joel would've picked up that knife. But at least now I know that it was him."

I was right there with her with wanting those answers.

"I see you with a cup in your hand. That's when answers will come."

I looked down at the paper cup in my hand. "Holy crap!"

Chapter Thirty-Six

Five hours later, Steve arrived at my door. "Well, that wasn't the way I expected to spend my Saturday morning."

While Fozzie danced at our feet, I gave Steve a quick kiss. "How'd it go? Did Detective Pearson take Joel into custody?"

"Yeah, shortly after you and your mom left. I'm sure he's getting booked into County as we speak."

"Did he actually confess?" I asked, heading into the kitchen since I knew he'd be hungry. "From what you told Amity while we were waiting for Detective Pearson to interview her, Joel was a little more talkative than when I called you."

"Most of it was spin and excuses while his girlfriend was there. The most that he'd admit was that it was an accident."

"An accidental knife to the heart?"

"Yeah, I know." Steve took a seat at the table and ran his hand over Fozzie's ear. "And he only went there to make a kiwi delivery—something Stillwell said he did on semi-regular basis. He insisted that the subject of the promissory note never even came up."

"Of course not." Although that did explain where all the kiwis I saw in that bowl came from.

"I'm sure his story will evolve over the next twenty-four hours. It usually does once they realize the trouble they're in."

I turned to Steve as I opened my refrigerator. "It's a good thing Amity found that note, because Joel Stillwell wasn't on my radar at all."

He smirked.

"Not that I was looking."

"Along with your granny. If she'd had her way, Pearson would have taken someone named Havens into custody."

"Well, she got a little caught up with the investigation since we were right next door when it happened."

"*She* got a little caught up?"

"Be nice and don't bite the hand trying to feed you." I grabbed a package of sliced cheddar. "How's grilled cheese sound?"

"That's fine. I'll take whatever you've got to offer."

Crossing the kitchen, I stepped over Fozzie so that I could sit in Steve's lap. "That's very accommodating of you. What if I want to offer some of this?" I pressed my lips to his while Fozzie whimpered his displeasure that he was being ignored.

"That's very nice." Steve nuzzled my neck and then abruptly stopped.

"What's wrong?"

"You smell like your mother."

Swell.

"She must have slimed me when she gave me a hug good-bye. I'll go change," I tried to push off him, but he held me tight.

"No need. I can take care of this." With an evil gleam in his eyes, Steve unbuttoned my daisy print camp shirt, pulled it off me, and then threw it into the other room.

He sniffed my bare shoulder. "Ah, much better. Now, what were you getting ready to offer me?"

"A cheese sandwich?"

"No, I think it was something after that," he said, working his way down the swell of my breast.

Maybe he wasn't so hungry after all.

Chapter Thirty-Seven

"This turned out to be a great day for a wedding," I said, dancing with Steve at Donna's wedding reception four weeks later. "When it started raining last night during the rehearsal, Donna thought it was a sign of things to come."

Steve held me close as we swayed to the Ed Sheeran hit that the disc jockey had selected for a slow dance. "Donna and her signs. I never realized she took that much stock in premonitions and signs."

Now wasn't the time to mention our visit to Harmony House. "It's more like she has an open mind about that stuff." And mine was considerably more open than it used to be. "But everything worked out okay."

And not just for Donna.

For Killian Havens, who drove away with Max in the shiny black pickup Amity wanted him to have.

For Killian's parents, who would soon be expanding their farm.

For the Constantines, who were happy to keep supplying what the local farms and gardens needed.

And maybe, the next time I ran into Amity, she'd be

able to smile, knowing that she made something good happen for the people she once called family.

"Yep." Steve held me a little tighter. "Sometimes, everything works out."

The venue at the lavender farm Donna and Ian selected had sure turned out to be the ideal location for an intimate wedding with family and friends. A lovely garden lush with blooms bordered a large patio under strings of festive lights while the setting sun lit wispy clouds aflame with pink and orange.

"She couldn't have asked for a more spectacular evening, and look how happy they are," I said, watching Donna and Ian dancing while Peyton danced next to them with Buddy in her arms.

"Who wouldn't be happy dancing with a dog wearing a bowtie?"

"I know. Makes me think I should start dressing Fozzie in formal wear."

"Oh?" Steve looked down at me. "Do you have some formal occasion in mind that the mutt and I should start planning for?"

The music stopped and my mouth went dry. "No. I was just...you know...talking about cute doggy stuff." And not another wedding. Absolutely, positively, not a wedding, because I kept sticking my foot in my mouth every time the subject came up.

Thank goodness there was a slight breeze because my strawberry chiffon bridesmaid dress had suddenly become very hot.

"Having fun?" Donna asked, rushing by with Buddy

chasing her train while Peyton pulled her by the hand.

I had been until that moment.

"Want to take a break?" Steve asked when an up-tempo song started playing.

A break to sip a little champagne with Rox and Eddie sitting at one of the tables and cool off? "You bet."

"Great."

Taking my hand, he set off on the footpath that cut through the middle of the garden. Not the direction I thought we were going to go but it smelled wonderful, and if our noses were busy, maybe our mouths wouldn't need to be.

"You got shortchanged yesterday," Steve said as we walked under an arbor of fragrant wisteria.

Shortchanged? "What are you talking about?"

"It was your birthday and you spent it getting rained on at a wedding rehearsal."

"You were here with me. We had a good time despite the rain."

Steve turned to me. "Yes, but I have something for you. I wanted to give it to you yesterday, but not out here in the rain."

"You gave me a present at the house, before we left." A framed photo of Fozzie that he took last December, when we went hiking in the mountains.

Steve pulled a small black box from his jacket pocket, got down on one knee, and opened the box, revealing a diamond solitaire ring. And all the air rushed out of my body.

"I've wanted to do this for a while. But I knew we

needed to take it slow. Considering I've known you since we were eight, we've taken it really slow. But I don't want to do that anymore. Charmaine, you're the one I want to see when I wake up in the morning—*every* morning. To keep doing what we're doing is wasting time." He smiled. "Wouldn't you agree?"

I would have been stupid to say anything but yes. "I love what we've been doing, but yes, I agree."

"I love you. Marry me."

I'm not stupid. I agreed to that, too.

THE END

ABOUT THE AUTHOR

Wendy Delaney writes fun-filled cozy mysteries and is the award-winning author of the Working Stiffs Mystery series. A long-time member of Mystery Writers of America, she's a Food Network addict and pastry chef wannabe. When she's not killing off story people she can be found on her treadmill, working off the calories from her latest culinary adventure.

Wendy lives in the Seattle area with the love of her life and is a proud grandma. For book news please visit her website at www.wendydelaney.com, email her at wendy@wendydelaney.com, and connect with her on Facebook at www.facebook.com/wendy.delaney.908.